Close to Home

A Collection of Short Stories,
Memoirs, Poetry, and Recipes

ISBN 978-1-62806-394-3 (print | paperback)
ISBN 978-1-62806-397-4 (print | hardback)
ISBN 978-1-62806-395-0 (ebook)

Library of Congress Control Number 2023922070

Published by Salt Water Media
29 Broad Street, Suite 104
Berlin, MD 21811
www.saltwatermedia.com

Cover images provided by the author

Close to Home

A Collection of Short Stories, Memoirs, Poetry, and Recipes

Faye Green

Other Books by Faye Green

Dedication

To my husband, Bill Byer, who arrived just in time

Instructions For Reading

CLOSE TO HOME

Keep this book near your favorite reading place.

When you have some reading time, bring a cup of something, and open the book.

Make a choice from the randomly arranged table of contents. Fiction or non-fiction? Very short, short, longer, very long?

Check the box so you know what you have read.

Email your star rating on each story, poem, or recipe: greenvine@verizon.net

Come back to your chair to make another choice and read again.

Come back to your chair to make
another choice and read again.

Come back to your chair to make
another choice and read again.

- fg

Dear Reader,

Thank you for picking up *Close to Home* to read today.

This collection is gathered and compiled from my head, desk, and computer. Some written recently when I decided to publish this book. Some written long ago and almost forgotten. It is surprising how story ideas stayed in my head so I could again use characters from novels written years ago. Suprising how many fractured works were in my files ready to be rewritten, edited, and bound. I have retrieved and published them so they would not be overlooked and lost someday when my office is cleaned out. I have a personal connection to every story, sequel, poem, and recipe contained in this book. Each one is close to my heart in some way. Each is an important part of my body of work. *Close to Home* is for my family, my family of friends, and my family of readers. It is a book for quiet times and quick diversions. Each piece stands alone. I hope you cannot decide which is your favorite—maybe it will be the next one you choose. It is my hope that you will know Faye Green, Author, better after reading *Close to Home*.

— **Faye**

Table of Contents

This story is a sequel to the book, *Gertie* (2014). The novel had two main characters—Gertie Morgan and Hilltop Manor. This novella brings both of those characters together again with focus on the manor, now known as:

Hilltop
Bed, Breakfast and Apple Pie Inn.
Laurel, Maryland. 1953

Hilltop

Chapter 1

Gretta Morgan, known by all as Gertie, walked down to the apple orchard to collect her thoughts as she often did in the early evening light. She left the huge, white mansion on the hill behind her and sat on the old bench, looking at the trees. Unlike the trees, full of bud, Hilltop mansion had finished its metamorphosis. It was now Hilltop Bed, Breakfast and Apple Pie Inn.

"Come on trees, give us apples so Bertha can make pies," she smiled as she commanded the orchard.

During the war, Gertie's Hilltop mansion was the USO outpost hosting men and women moving from Ft George G Meade to England, to Normandy, and to the European front. The mansion continued through the war and after, hosting the able wounded recovering at the post hospital and Walter Reed Hospital. In the intervening years Gertie's door was open to a constant stream of veterans who had come to Hilltop USO during the war. They were always welcomed back to the stately home and beautiful grounds.

The idea to make a Bed & Breakfast of the beautiful mansion bloomed gradually. She hired Maggie Stone to manage it. Her directions to Maggie were specific: No service person, man or woman, or family member, who had been to Hilltop during the war, would pay to stay at Hilltop Bed, Breakfast and Apple Pie Inn.

"We won't make any profit," Maggie responded.

"I want to continue the service Hilltop began in 1942. Visits from veterans and their families will dwindle as time goes by. Count the pennies, Maggie. I'm not concerned about profit—just flour, sugar, butter, and maybe eggs," Gertie concluded on a light note. "Bertha is more than happy to continue her life in the kitchen here—cooking breakfasts and baking apple pies. I'm hiring staff for the house and grounds."

During the war and in the recovery years after, Hilltop Manor had been a beacon of light when the world was truly dark. Gertie loved seeing uniformed young men and women on the grounds, dancing in the great room, singing on the staircase and eating Bertha's treats. Secretly she hoped many more would find their way, in peace, back to her door.

The B & B was successful in Gertie's eyes, not so in Maggie's. After four years, many unpaid guests and too few paying ones, Hilltop barely managed to pay for flour, sugar, butter, and maybe eggs. Gertie was happy to pay wages and maintenance with profits from Hilltop's surrounding farmland, orchards, and her sizable wealth.

She got up from the orchard bench and walked back to the manse with her reverie lighting her steps.

Maggie met her on the side porch with a face full of alarm.

"Gertie, I was on my way to get you. We have a problem waiting in the foyer."

Gertie loved Maggie's alarms because they always came with absolute confidence that her boss would know what to do.

"OK, Mag. Who's in the foyer?"

"A boy. Bertha is watching him. He's skinny; looks about thirteen and *di.err..tee.*" Maggie drew a breath. "Probably hungry, too."

"Hilltop Bed and Breakfast and Apple Pie Inn. A customer?" Gertie smiled.

"Hardly."

The boy was as Maggie described except more so. He could be Caucasian but was so soiled Gertie was not sure. Mud-caked hair that pushed out of a baseball cap appeared to be red. *Or was it colored by Maryland clay?* His clothes were damp, obviously from this morning's shower. A closer look showed that he was trembling.

"My name is Gertie Morgan, and this is Maggie Stone. And what is your name, young man?"

"Lee."

"Your parent's names?"

"Mary Ann and Johnny."

"Last name?"

Silence.

"I'll go," he offered and turned to the door.

Gertie thought fast to assess what was happening. Surely, fright and wet clothes caused his shivers. She put her arm around his filthy, wet shoulders and drew him close. "Lee, before you go, we would like to give you something to eat. Hungry?"

"Yes, ma'am." His hungry eyes looked across the foyer, into the library and up the beautiful staircase. "Is that the library?" He asked before his eyes rested unwavering on Gertie and smiled. His smiling eyes went to Gertie's soul, and she thought of the needy servicemen who looked up at her the same way from hospital beds during the war. Lee No-Last-Name had the same quiet confidence in her... and hope.

Yes, hope, she thought.

While the dirty boy made a 360-degree turn to see all he could, Gertie took charge.

"Bertha, please fix sandwiches and pie for us. Maggie, call Sam. Lee can go take a bath and get clean clothes at the farmhouse. I think he's about Sam, Jr.'s size. Ask Sam to meet him at the stable."

She walked Lee to the kitchen door and pointed at the stable. "Go ahead, now. My brother or one of his boys will meet you. Things will be so much better after you clean up and come back to this kitchen and eat. Won't they?"

Lee did not say a word; he just did as he was told.

Gertie and Maggie watched Lee slowly walk across the lower lawn toward the stable, each lost in thought at this strange turn of events in what had started out to be a quiet spring evening.

"Maggie, I need to talk to Sheriff Wallace. Would you get him on the phone? I think we have a runaway on our hands." Maggie went toward the phone brushing dirt off her hands from touching the boy.

Gertie washed up and waited for Maggie to bring the phone. "Yes, Pete. It's Gertie Morgan."

"What can I do for you, Gertie?"

"We have a young boy who came to Hilltop's doorstep. Most likely a runaway."

"I'll come right out and get…"

"No, no, Pete," she interrupted. "Don't come. It's Friday; it's past dinner time. Give us a chance to feed him and see if he will tell us anything. Don't you agree, he is better off here?"

"I don't know if I agree or not. We can't take any chances. I don't want you in danger. How old is he? Did you get his name?"

"We guess twelve or thirteen. Only his first name—Lee. Don't worry about our safety. He's just a child and Sam is here."

"Gertie, I don't like it, but I will wait until tomorrow to

come. Try to get his last name and at least the state where he hails from. Meanwhile I'll check the surrounding states for a missing person bulletin. I'll see you in the morning."

Maggie poured two cups of coffee as they settled at the table to wait.

"Did he knock at the door or ask any questions?" Gertie asked.

"No. He must have been sitting against the door. I heard a shuffle and opened the door. He kinda fell in and rolled onto the carpet."

"Strange." Gertie was mystified by the dirty boy that acted like he belonged at Hilltop.

Bertha had sandwiches and potato salad ready by the time Lee came back up the hill with Sam.

"Gertie, step out on the porch a minute." Sam needed to talk to his sister. "I assume you're going to put him up overnight. But I insist, not in the house with you and Bertha. Too many *ifs*. He's just a kid. Suppose we keep him at the farmhouse and let him bunk in with Sammy."

"Alright, Sam. I'll send him back to the farmhouse after he eats."

Lee ate with great relish. Gertie and Maggie watched in amazement as he devoured two sandwiches, two helpings of potato salad and anxiously awaited the pie.

"I'll bet that's apple pie."

Gertie nodded.

"Thought so," Lee replied as he accepted the plate, fork, and sweet, gooey treat.

That was the extent of conversation during the meal. His mouth was too busy. Lee's eyes were busy, too. He constantly looked around at his surroundings. At last, he drew his napkin across his mouth and chin and pushed his chair back.

"Thank you. I should leave but I don't have my clothes…"

Suddenly, as if his brain kicked in after his stomach was full, he stood in alarm. "My clothes! The lady..." he breathlessly exclaimed while pointing to the farmhouse. "...she's going to wash them." Lee bolted from the table and raced to the door. "Oh, no..." he cried as he jumped from the top step and ran as if his life depended on his race across the lawn to the farmhouse. Sam heard the beating on his door and answered the alarm.

"Lee! What's wrong?"

My pockets...," he was out of breath. "Some things in my pockets..." His head bounced back and forth as if he did not know where to go, where to look, where to run. Lee fell to his knees. "Where are my pants?" It was more than a question, he was pleading.

Sam calmed Lee with assuring tones. "My wife washed your clothes. They are still wet, Lee."

"I had some things in the pockets..." The devastated look on the boy's face tore at Sam.

"Sit down," Sam directed. "My wife has a lot of experience washing boys' pants. I doubt anything in your pocket went through the wash." He turned to his son. "Sammy, come talk to Lee while I find your mother."

Lee did as he was told and tried to relax but he never took his eyes off the doorway that Sam passed through to find his wife. He watched the doorway until Sam returned with a large, tattered envelope and a small paper bag, intact. Lee came to his feet, resisting the urge to run and grab his treasures from Sam's hand.

"These?"

"Yes, sir."

"Sleep here tonight, bunk in with Sammy—your choice, across the foot of his bed or on the floor. Your clothes will be dry by mid-morning. I doubt they will dry overnight but they are on the line for the morning sun. You ok?"

"Yes, sir," he said again as he refolded the big envelope and slid it, with the other items, into the borrowed pants' pocket. Then he took time to look in the bag and stuffed it in another pocket. "The floor will be fine, thank you. I'll go back up to the manor to thank Miss Gertie for dinner. I was rude when I ran out." He went toward the door and turned. "Actually, I like the floor." The atmosphere was relaxed from the crisis of minutes ago. A grin lit his face, piling freckles up in a heap on his wrinkled nose. "I'll be back."

"Polite boy," Sam said to his children, as an example, as soon as Lee left.

Lee walked halfway up the lawn and sat on the cool grass. He opened the envelope to make sure everything was still there. The bag was checked in the same way. He considered running to the road and disappearing, but he didn't because the clothes he was wearing were not his. "I have to stay tonight—have to." He admitted to himself, "I'm glad." *At least tonight,* he thought as he resumed his walk to the house, glancing to his left where the apple trees stood in lines, just as they were supposed to be.

Gertie had seen enough to know the boy was bright, well brought up and not a threat to anyone at Hilltop. "Tomorrow Lee and I will have a heart to heart," she explained to the mirror. She decided to be direct and honest with him before Pete came in the morning. *But first, a good night's sleep.*

* * *

Five days ago, Lee's fate was the topic of discussion before going to his mother's funeral. The four-room bungalow's small kitchen hardly had room for his seven relatives. His cousins and uncles—all McDougals—shared two six-packs and talked as if he was not on the other side of the paper-thin walls. It was clear; no one wanted him.

It was even clearer to Lee—he didn't want them either.

"I'll get his Greyhound ticket to St. Louis. You got Emma's address?" Lee recognized Uncle Paddy's voice and attitude.

"Yeah."

"Write it down for him. She's his grandmother. It's only right. When this place is sold, I'll get my money back for the ticket. Don't forget."

"How could we forget? You'll harp on it until you get it."

"This dump ain't worth much but it should pay the doctor, the funeral home and that ticket."

"Emma'll take Lee in...but we better not tell her before he gets there. Best if he just shows up at her door. Agreed?"

"Agreed." Another round of beer settled his fate. "Emma ain't gonna take this easy. Best if she doesn't have a choice. What's she gonna do if he's there? She can't afford no tickets to send him back." Uncle Paddy had it all figured out.

"If there's any money left, I'll send it to her for Lee." Lee's favorite cousin said the only kind thing uttered that night.

Lee wrote a note and left it on the table before they went to the funeral. Easy. Granny Emma did not know he was coming; A quick one-line lie would take care of everything.

I am leaving for St. Louis after the funeral. Goodbye.
    Lee

Lee knew his relatives would believe what they wanted to believe. Uncle Paddy would be glad he didn't have to buy a ticket. Everyone could go home and stop worrying about Lee. Besides, it wasn't a complete lie. He had to pass St. Louis to get to Maryland.

There was only one person who would understand why he could not live in St. Louis, and she died day before yesterday. His mother knew he hated the city and dirty tenement where his grandmother lived. Life was hard enough without Daddy all these years. Lee could not face life without his mother if he had to live in a dirty city tenement surrounded by concrete.

Lee didn't want to go to St. Louis, and he didn't want to take anything from Missouri, either. He needed to be on rolling hills, green expanse and he needed to breathe clean air when he let his mother go and finally saw his father's grave.

Lee stood beside his mother's grave. He watched the funeral director pile the flower baskets on the mound before the pastor said his final words. Spring was already hot in the Missouri town. The sun wilted the flowers and tested the patience of the dozen mourners who wanted to move on—none of them more than Lee. He refused the offer of a ride back to the house with his second cousin and great uncle. The other cousins from Iowa and two more uncles could gather in the four-room bungalow and eat some church casseroles, but not the orphaned son. Lee picked up some Missouri black dirt from the mound beside his mother's grave, put it in a large envelope and walked to the highway that cut the town in half. He pushed it in with the items he took from home and patted his full pockets.

He was well dusted with road grime as he counted the sixteen-wheelers that passed. "One. Two. Three. Four…" Finally, the seventh big rig hit the brakes and pulled to the side.

"Hey, kid. You better have a good reason to be out on this highway, hitching east bound."

"My mother died," was all the boy said. The driver assumed she died back east.

"Hop in. I'm going as far as Indianapolis."

That would help. Indianapolis was halfway to Hilltop Manor.

Chapter 2

JOHN LEE McDOUGAL

John Lee McDougal aka Johnny McDougal was a rough-ie. He fought his way through grade school and was about to scuff and scratch through high school. He had learned a lot in fifteen years, mostly, if you want it, you have to fight for it. His red hair bled down to his face when he was mad. Johnny became all one color in anger and most kids yielded to him. It was his red hair that put him on this path. He was the subject of laughter and teasing. *Carrot Top* was a terrible name in the first grade. When a school bully, Willy Klopik, came out of his third-grade classroom and pushed young Johnny McDougal and called him *stupid-freckled-strawberry*, rage spilled over. Johnny was big for his age and the two combatants were close to the same size. John beat Willy in a fight that could never have been called fair, what with Willy being almost two years older—but the bully was not a fighter. He was all talk and John smashed his mouth with his fist, cut his lip and drew blood with his first, and only, blow.

From that day on, Johnny embraced his exceptional size, the value of fighting and the special importance of the first blow.

When he got home the story of his fight with a third grader had already come to the McDougal household by way of Johnny's three older siblings. Emma McDougal's only remark as she passed the potato soup was, "Am I going to get a call from school? Hold your bowl, Johnny."

"I think so, Ma. It happened in the hallway." Sally answered as she dropped a cracker in her soup. "Johnny, you gotta learn—don't fight in the school so they don't call Ma."

"Maybe they won't call. It happened so fast and was over

before Mrs. Banning got there." Wayne offered his opinion as he bit his bread dripping with soup.

"Suppose Willy tells or his parents come to school about his split lip. Then you will get a call tomorrow, Ma." Colin put his bowl down. "I betcha. More soup?"

Emma left the table and her four older children to feed the twins at the kitchen counter. Her day was busy enough with work and worry without having to face a call from school for Johnny. *First grade and already trouble*, she thought as she mashed the potatoes in the soup for the twins, Tommy and Patrick. The debate was continuing at the table between Johnny, Sally, Colin and Wayne but their mother had tuned them out. Finally, when the commotion among the children got loud, she banged her spoon against the soup pot. "Enough!" she cried. "Wayne, you and Colin go to the tavern and get your father before there is no money left to even buy milk and potatoes."

It was a grubby existence for the McDougal family. On this day, Johnny had discovered how he was going to deal with it.

The bully was defeated; long live the new bully. Johnny didn't have the bully mentality and did not seek confrontation. But, after beating Willy, the children in the elementary school stepped aside for him and he came to expect it. Johnny was Goliath and he was only six years old.

The following Saturday when the boys were lined up to get their hair cut, Johnny rebelled.

"No. I don't want my hair cut."

"Johnny, I'm cutting that curly mop. Get over here, boy." His mother demanded.

John ran away for two days. Emma let it go. Fighting with her son about his hair was not worth energy that she did not have, especially seven months pregnant.

His red hair grew to a thick and curly mop as his mother predicted. It was a dare that he wore to school every day. He

11

didn't hurt anyone, but he pushed kids around and they gave him room. The result was no one called him names or made any reference to his red hair. His fellow students stepped aside, yielded when they stood in line, and stayed out of his way. The other result was Johnny had no friends.

He brought his attitude home. His brothers and sister gave him plenty of room, too. He did not have to demand anything—it was simply given to him in favor of peace. Soon he was sent alone to get his father from the tavern. Even the old man did what the big, huge headed red-haired boy asked.

"Pa, time to go home."

"Aye." The older version of young John downed his pint quickly and followed the boy home.

* * *

Johnny's life changed one cool fall day. It seemed a normal day, in fact it was in every way until he pushed a boy off the path so he could pass.

"John McDougal, you are a big headed, carrot-top bully." The words came fast and furious. "I'm sick of you." He turned to see what idiot dared to challenge him. Suddenly, his twisting body was slammed with enough force to send him to the ground. He did not even have time to break his fall so his face went into the dirt, disturbed by his twisting feet and his assailant's swift kick in the dirt dusted his face. Dirt was in his hair, in his mouth, in his teeth and in his eyes. Rage was turning his face and neck blood red and even his hair seemed more crimson. His freckles were lost in the grime. "You better run fast or you will be eating this dirt!" He gathered a handful.

Johnny looked up to see two shapely ankles standing defiantly. "I'm not going anywhere, John McDougal. I'm not afraid of a handful of dirt!" The voice was no longer angry. It was laughing and it was beguilingly feminine.

That was the moment when Johnny McDougal fell in love with Mary Ann Brogan. He didn't know what to do with the feeling passing through his vulnerable spread-eagle body covered with dirt.... so he did something ridiculous, he put the handful of dirt in his pocket. John sat and watched her walk deliberately, arrogantly, like an angel, into the school. He sat there for almost an hour, but he did not waste the time. He thought.

When he presented himself in the office to get a tardy slip, he was a different person. The outward changes did not come quickly. His hair remained uncut and his life at school was isolated but inside he was changing. Johnny was no longer focused on himself and small satisfactions and unsavory habits. He woke up thinking of Mary Ann each day.

Johnny combed his hair with water to tame the curl and he kept his clothes folded so they were neater when he wore them. Three days later they passed in the hallways, he smiled at her and to his amazement, she smiled back. Johnny didn't suddenly begin being nice to everyone. He did not know how to be helpful. No, he just stopped doing unkind things. He wasn't friendly; he wasn't hurtful. He wasn't soft-spoken; he just didn't say anything. He wasn't aggressive; he just started letting the world go by. Each day in itself was remarkable. Johnny McDougal had decided—he was sick of himself, too.

It took almost a month to get the courage to speak to Mary Ann, even on the same dirt path where they met.

"Hey!" Mary Ann turned around with a quizzical look on her face. She didn't say anything, so he had to start the conversation. "Today is my sixteenth birthday." It was stupid and dumb to say that. *Oh, God, I should die.*

"Mine, too." Mary Ann replied in amazement.

"Really?"

"Really, John McDougal." She walked away. He struggled to breathe.

Ten seconds passed as she moved away down the path. Mary Ann stopped and in unison they shouted to each other. "Happy Birthday!"

Mary Ann Brogan lived in the biggest house in town. Her father was a famous author of western novels. Her life was gentle and kind, and rich. The family of four gathered in the huge dining room each evening when the five o'clock whistle blew. Sadie, the maid, served a hot and healthy meal that had been prepared by Effie, the cook.

Maude Brogan believed dinner had to settle before dessert, so Harold Brogan brought the St. Louis Dispatch to the table so a lively discussion could fill the hour before Sadie came with her dessert tray. Harold led with the headlines. Maude liked to point out the latest innovations from advertisers. Mary Ann liked to open the funnies and follow Little Lulu while her brother, Sean, waited patiently to talk about Enos Slaughter, Johnny Mize and the Cardinals.

This household was 180 degrees different from the McDougals scrapping for dinner down in their four-room house across the Santa Fe railroad tracks.

For dessert Mary Ann had ice cream and oatmeal cookies with raisins. Johnny had a second ladle of thin potato soup which was good if Emma had an onion, and if he wanted it.

At dinner time, Maude called her husband down from his typewriter in the loft office.

Across town, Emma never knew if her husband had worked today at the fur company, if he was at the Town Tavern, or even if he would come home.

* * *

It was not out of Johnny's way to walk down Gilbert Avenue, pass the Brogans' big Victorian home sitting in the middle of a wide green lawn. He could make a right turn at the end of Gilbert and cross the railroad tracks on South Fourth Street. Johnny just never chose that route before today.

"Hey, wait up." He called and caught up with her before they were off the school grounds.

"Well, John McDougal, what shall we talk about?" She asked immediately when he fell into step with her.

"Are you always going to call me by both of my names? Everybody else just calls me Johnny."

"Mmm." She looked up into his green eyes. "No, John McDougal. I'm going to call you Johnny, starting tomorrow."

"Good."

"Are you going to call me, *Hey*? That's all I've heard from you. Maybe you don't even know my name."

"Mary," he teased with a pause. "Ann." His smile was a dazzling grin.

They both laughed and walked along in a comfortable silence bought with the humorous banter. At her walkway, he said, "Tomorrow. Same time. Same place."

* * *

Johnny and Mary Ann went into their senior year, 1941, as special friends. They walked and talked. Each waited for the other when class schedules crossed. At football games she cheered for him—loud and excited. When the gang gathered at the soda fountain, they managed to sit side by side at the counter. It was fun and it was good but there were stresses that prevented them from being boyfriend and girlfriend. Nothing kept them from being *friends*.

Walking home on the first Friday in December, Mary Ann

started the conversation she had rehearsed in her room for a week.

"Johnny, would you come to meet my parents? Saturday?" It was a logical progression and blending of their lives.

"No."

His one-word answer was unexpected, but she assumed Saturday was not a good day.

"OK, we can make it another day. You haven't said anything about the Christmas dance next month. I want to go with you. But, I can't if you don't meet my parents."

"No." His voice was soft, and his face went pasty. His answer was not meant to be harsh. Both his countenance and voice were full of pain and regret.

"No? On everything?" Mary Ann was searching for understanding and nothing in her life helped her to assess what he was refusing to do.

Johnny took her hand and drew her to the far side of the huge chestnut tree at the corner of Third Street. He took off his coat, plopped himself down and pulled her to sit on his coat. In the few moments it took to get settled in this quiet secluded spot, he had time to find the first sentence of something he needed to say.

"Mary Ann, haven't you wondered why I haven't brought up the dance? Wondered why I haven't even taken your hand or tried to kiss you?"

Her eyes grew big, and she wondered if this was the moment that she had waited for.

"You must know I want to."

Kiss me! Now! My friends have at least been kissed by now. Mary Ann's mind raged.

His head was down, and he made no movement to come closer.

Her whole body slumped in disappointment. Her silence invited him to go on.

16

"We have to stay friends. I can't come into your world, and you absolutely, positively cannot come into mine. That's the way it is."

Mary Ann started to speak but he put his finger to her lips. His first personal touch caused her to draw a quick breath. Her lips burned and quivered where his finger had touched.

"I'm a McDougal. There are a million reasons why I live over by the Santa Fe tracks just like there are a million reasons why you live up here on Gilbert Avenue. I know who I am and who I'm gonna be." He paused for emphasis. "You are a Brogan. Look, Mary Ann, your big, beautiful house stands above the trees. I can see it from here." He pointed so she could not deny. "You're full of possibilities...and you have no idea who or what you are going to be some day. When I graduate in May, I will sort mink and muskrat furs at the company and try to help Mom and the kids. When you graduate, you will go to college." He stopped to let his words sink into Mary Ann's brain.

She looked up to him as he said, "I ain't gonna let a kiss or a dance take you off your path. I ain't!"

While he was deciding to get up from the grass and run the rest of the way home, Mary Ann leaned forward and kissed Johnny.

"Can you meet me at the movie on Sunday? The matinee?" Mary Ann asked Johnny for their first real date.

Wild horses would not keep Johnny from meeting Mary Ann, taking her hand and leading her into the movie on Sunday, December 7, 1941. Hormones were raging in the teenage boy, and he had no resistance after their first kiss. All his reason and common sense evaporated. He could hardly remember - much less recite - their differences.

"Sunday, matinee," he agreed.

Nothing can ruin that perfect day.

Chapter 3

LEE

Gertie was up early, seeking the coffee she could smell and the company of Bertha in the kitchen. The quiet of the Howard County hills soothed the wrinkles from her brow.

"Mornin', Bertha. Any stirring from the farmhouse?"

"I saw Mr. Sam at the stable and then leave."

"Ah, routine, even on a Saturday morning. I love it. Will I be content on Monday, my first day of retirement?" It was a question, but Bertha knew Gertie did not expect an answer from her.

"Look, Miss Gertie. Here come da dirty boy 'cross de lawn. He clean and shiny. What's his name agin?"

"Lee."

He knocked softly on the door.

"Come in, Lee. Had your breakfast?"

"Mrs. MacGregor offered but I had imposed too much. I'm wearing Sammy's clothes, and they gave me a place to sleep. Couldn't take breakfast, too."

"Bertha, breakfast for us, please." She turned and looked at Lee. "You'll eat or hurt our feelings, right Bertha?"

"Yes'm."

Breakfast was pleasant and Lee seemed totally at ease. The time was quickly approaching when difficult subjects had to be broached. Pete Wallace would be here as promised this morning.

"Lee, do you realize you cannot stay here without us telling your family and we cannot let you go alone out into the world again? It would help so much if you would share your story with me instead of the authorities."

"I don't want to cause you any trouble."

"Does that mean you will answer some questions for me?"

"Can't I just go?" He put his fork full of scrambled eggs back on the plate. "Please." His voice was pleading, and emotion-driven, but there were no signs that he would cry. Lee was exuding strength and determination. Gertie sensed that if he were detained or sent back to where he didn't want to be, he would run again to go wherever he *needed* to go.

"Lee," she placed her hand over his, "Sheriff Wallace will be here soon. Let me be on your side. I will help if I can."

"I know you will."

And how do you know that? Gertie wondered.

"Your last name, Lee. Are you ready to tell me?" Gertie began

Lee remained silent

"Where is home?" Gertie began again.

"Missouri. LaPlata, Missouri. It is a small town north of St. Louis. Macon County."

"Is that where your parents live?"

"My parents are dead."

"You *are* telling me the truth, aren't you? I would rather you not answer… than lie. Lee?"

"Miss Gertie, I will not lie. Not to you."

"Eat your breakfast. Finish your eggs. We will talk after you finish, son." Gertie concentrated on her plate, forcing food when her appetite was gone. She had hoped the resolution would come with a phone call to Lee's parents. More answers seemed to bring more problems.

Lee followed Gertie to the porch overlooking the orchard. He took a seat and settled back as if he was ready to talk.

"My father died nine years ago. My mother died a week ago last Tuesday. I left right after her funeral. They said I had to go live with my grandmother in St. Louis but…." His voice trailed off and his eyes looked into the distance.

"Who are *they*?"

"My cousins and uncles. Relatives who came to the funeral from Iowa and Chicago. I have a grandmother in St Louis. My Dad's mother. You see, I can't live in St. Louis with Grandma Emma. She doesn't want me, either. I left and solved a lot of problems out there, but it looks like I brought them to Hilltop." With that thought, Lee began to weep. It was the first tears he'd shed since his mother said goodbye. Amid his silent tears, he said, "I'm so sorry, Miss Gertie. I don't want to cause you and Hilltop any trouble. Please, let me get my clothes and go."

"No, Lee. I can't let you go." She went to him and offered her shoulder.

"Sheriff Wallace is checking for missing persons. I have to tell him to call Missouri."

"No one is looking for me. There won't be any bulletins. Grandma Emma didn't know I was coming and the relatives at the funeral think that's where I went." His voice was tragically sad when he said, "Nobody's looking for me." His crying ended but tears continued to quietly sneak out the corners of his eyes.

"Lee, I have to know your last name. Please."

"McDougal."

"Your parents?"

"John and Mary Ann McDougal."

"Here comes Sheriff Wallace in the drive. Go down to the farmhouse and wait until your clothes are dry. I'll see if you can stay here until some of this is sorted out. Agreed? You won't run away, promise?"

"I promise," Lee answered. "Can I ask one thing, Miss Gertie. Will you do one thing for me?"

She nodded, "If I can."

I want to visit Arlington Cemetery before you send me back. Is that too far? Is that too much to ask before I'm sent back to Missouri?"

"Unless your grandmother objects, I will."

"She won't."

Gertie turned her attention to Pete Wallace coming around the house.

"Morning, Gertie. I thought I'd find you on the porch."

"Good morning, Pete." She greeted as she pointed to Lee crossing the lawn. "His name is Lee McDougal. Parents, John and Mary Ann McDougal from LaPlata, Missouri. He said his mother died a week or so ago, and his father has been dead nine years."

"That will be easy to check. Any family looking for him?"

"He says not. There is a grandmother in St. Louis named Emma. I assume last name McDougal."

Pete was writing it all down. "His age?"

"I forgot to ask. I will. He looks at least twelve, maybe thirteen, but is very wise for his age. Could be older."

Pete continued to make notes as he looked up. "Where's he headed?"

"I think Virginia. He asked me to take him to Arlington National Cemetery before sending him back. Maybe his father died in the war and that's where he is buried. Just dawned on me. Nine years ago is 1944." Gertie let that thought tie into all she knew about Lee McDougal. "Funny thing, Pete. It almost seems he was coming to Hilltop. Not an accident that he was on our porch." More thoughts swam in her head as she realized vocalizing the idea made it stronger and more obvious. Gertie wanted to talk to Lee again—on new topics.

"Really. Well, Gertie, we can't assume anything. I'll have to get more answers from him. He's at the farmhouse?" Pete started for the door.

"Pete, could you write your questions and leave it to me? This boy is fragile, and I don't want him to bolt and run. Can we keep him here while you sort this out? I think soon he will be ready to talk to you."

"I will give this another day but no longer. We have a responsibility to his family, and I have an obligation. Talk to him and get him ready to talk to me tomorrow. Meanwhile I will contact authorities in this Missouri town and try to locate his grandmother."

"Pete…. Tomorrow is Sunday. Could you come back Monday?" She pleaded with her eyes and Sheriff Wallace had to smile.

"I'll call tomorrow and come back Monday afternoon. I probably can't start getting answers until Monday morning anyway." Pete Wallace easily went back to his official position. "Monday, Gertie," he cautioned.

"Thanks, Pete. We are going to take him to Arlington tomorrow."

Chapter 4

JOHN LEE McDOUGAL and MARY ANN BROGAN

The cool December early evening was teeming with excitement when Johnny and Mary Ann left the theater. People were milling about on Main Street, and more than the usual numbers were out of their houses.

"Did I hear someone say *attack?*" Mary Ann asked.

"I don't know. There's my brother." Johnny raised his voice to stop Colin on his bike. "Colin! Hey, over here."

"Johnny, have you heard?" Colin put one foot down to hold the bicycle. "The Japs bombed Pearl Harbor. It's war. FDR is going to speak. I've got to get home to the radio."

"Pick me up at Gilbert. I'm walking Mary Ann home, then I'll ride your handlebars. I want to hear, too."

"OK, get a move on. I don't want to miss it."

As he rode the handlebars down past the Santa Fe station, Johnny had one thought. *I won't be sorting furs, if President Roosevelt says war, I'm going in the Army.*

Of course, Roosevelt did declare war. All three of the McDougal boys announced they would sign up.

"I can't stop you, Wayne and Colin, but Johnny...you are not of age," Ma asserted.

"But you and Pop can sign for me," Johnny could not accept her answer. True, he was the youngest, but he was the biggest and strongest of the McDougal boys. Johnny could not imagine being left out of this fight.

"I've got to have one of you here. Can't let you all go."

Johnny was disappointed beyond belief. He stormed out and did not come back for three days. When he came back, Wayne met him at the door with news.

"I'm 4F, Johnny. Deaf from Pop's beating. I can't go in the army."

"I'll go in your place, Wayne. I'll kick the Japs and Germans all over the world. Where's Ma?"

It was easy to get the signed permission to join up. Almost as easy as making the decision to go. The hard part would be telling Mary Ann goodbye. Mary Ann had given his life meaning and now he was going to war. Johnny knew she loved him just as he loved her. Johnny and Mary Ann had not declared their love, but they would before Johnny got on the bus to leave.

"Mary Ann, this could be our future. I'll do good in the army and when the war is over, I will be trained to do something more than set in LaPlata and sort furs. You'll see."

She didn't see. All she could say was, "Oh, Johnny," and cling to him.

Two weeks later they faced their final hours together.

"Can you spend my last night with me, Mary Ann? We'll go over to the Santa Fe Lake. I'll bring blankets."

"I have to sneak out."

"I'll meet you behind our chestnut tree. Wear a warm coat. What time?"

"As soon after eleven as I can."

They walked without talking down Gilbert Avenue, across the train tracks, past Fourth Street, down the unpaved road to the lake. The night was cold and clear. Stars seemed to number in the millions as the two children wrapped in blankets and began to talk the night away.

Who knows what brought passion under the blanket for Mary Ann and Johnny as the black night shrunk their world down to twenty-four square feet beside Santa Fe Lake? Was it the normal hormones of two seventeen-year-olds, or was it the pending separation? Was it terror about Johnny going to war, or was it fear of facing every day in LaPlata without him? Was Mary Ann too willing? Was Johnny too demanding?

Under covers, without consequences, this couple, like couples all over the world, were taking a big slice of happiness before God-only-knows-what. When there is no future promised and no dreams certain, pressing bodies together erases obligations and suspends impending disasters.

"We will have this," she whispered in longing ears. Young girls without rings, and young boys with nothing to offer, ride a crest that does not require a tomorrow.

"I'm sorry, Mary Ann." He cried several tears as he tried to apologize.

"Don't Johnny. It was no more you than me." She had no tears or apologies. In recalling the moments later, Mary Ann could not find the order of events. She only knew they both did what they both wanted to do.

"I leave in the morning…I wish we had time to get married. I would like to get on the bus knowing you are mine, Mary Ann."

"I'm yours, Johnny. Now and forever."

She took his hand in her hands and looked into eyes glowing with love. "With this ring, I thee wed." A birthstone ring slid off her right hand and onto his little finger past the second knuckle.

Johnny slid the ring back off his finger and put it on her left ring finger. "With this ring, I thee wed."

"You are my husband and I love you."

"You are my wife and I love you."

They fell back on the blanket laughing like the children they were. The rest of the night they talked and called each other *husband* and *wife*, continually breaking into giggles.

After the sun lit the eastern sky but before it broke the horizon, the newlyweds engaged in intercourse again. This time it was with angry passion and anxiety. She held him tighter; he pushed harder. She grasped his shoulder and let her fingers press his flesh. He lifted her under him with superhuman strength so that she was levitated to him. Mary Ann did not belong to the earth. She was suspended for a moment—totally Johnny's. They were one beyond gravity and the laws of the universe.

Reality has its own laws. Johnny was a soldier. Mary Ann was a schoolgirl. Neither one knew anything about reality when they walked to the Greyhound bus depot the next day.

"We've said it all…" he whispered, "wife."

Mary Ann took the ring from her finger and pushed it again past two knuckles on his little finger. "Keep our wedding ring, it will bring you home to me."

"I've nothing to leave with you, Mary Ann."

Little did he know that he had left her with a miniscule, fertilized egg that was traveling to her uterus.

Johnny's letters were full of love and missing her and they came with regularity. The mail man teased her about his load and Johnny's fault in it. Mary Ann's letters flew back to Johnny, but they were more contrived. She had to be careful what she told him. Writing them was not easy. She did not want to tell him she was pregnant.

The Brogans did not take her announcement six weeks later very calmly. This was a scandalous embarrassment for a family of prominence. The usual *shotgun* wedding could not be accomplished. After days of deliberations and plans, Mary Ann's parents called her to the parlor.

"Mary Ann, sit down."

Harold and Maude wasted no time. They came right to the point. "You will go to Aunt Sarah in Iowa City. The baby will be offered for adoption. We have arranged a correspondence school for your diploma so you can go to college the next term."

Mary Ann had gone through weeks of anguish as her body gave her the news. That anguish was minor compared to the outline prepared by her parents.

"Please, I want this baby. I want to marry Johnny. I'll do it all—go to Aunt Sarah, get my high school diploma, go to college. But I can't give away this baby."

"You do not have that choice. We will not bring that baby to this house."

"I love Johnny," she proclaimed as Harold Brogan struck his daughter for the first time in her life and ran from the room aghast at what he had done.

Mary Ann sat stoically, rubbed the redness on her face and said, "I'll not give this baby up, Mother. Nothing you or Father say or do can make me give up my baby. When Johnny comes home, we will marry."

Finally, she wrote the letter that had to be written. Johnny needed to know.

Johnny arranged to come home after boot camp. The Army made a 24-hour allowance due to the circumstance. A small ceremony in the Christian Church officially made Mary Ann Brogan and John McDougal man and wife.

Harold and Maude Brogan did not attend. They sat in their big mansion on Gilbert Street and never spoke of their daughter again.

Mary Ann took her swelled body over the Santa Fe tracks to live with the McDougals on meager food and Johnny's letters.

Johnny reported to Ft. Meade, Maryland. His first assignment. Some of his many letters told Mary Ann about Hilltop Manor USO. *My home away from home,* he wrote.

LEE

Chapter 5

Early Sunday morning, Gertie called Maggie. "Get the storage box with all the USO guest books. I need to know if John or Johnny McDougal from Missouri signed in."

"Gertie, you know how many we have!"

"I know, but I think Lee's father may have been here. It will solve some of the mystery. When I get back, I'll start looking through them. Monday. I have the time. I'm taking him to Arlington Cemetery today."

"Pete called. Emma McDougal doesn't have a listed phone number," Maggie reported.

Lee put on his fresh washed clothes and prepared for the special day when he would go to Arlington Cemetery. He walked up from the farmhouse and sat patiently on the step to wait for the appointed hour and Gertie. She found him there.

"Lee, did you have breakfast?"

"Yes, Ma'am."

"My driver will take us. It is a long drive. Plenty of time for you to tell me why you need to go to Arlington." As they walked, she placed her hand on his shoulder. Gertie left no doubt. Lee knew he had to tell.

Before they got in the limousine, Bertha rushed out with a lunch basket. "You be needin' this. Come home for dinner."

The beautiful Maryland countryside flew past the window as they headed south on Route 29 toward Washington, DC. "We do not pass through the historical parts of Washington today. When we cross the large river, it is the Potomac, and we will be in Virginia. Arlington is right there." She finished her travel spiel and invited Lee to talk with her silence and her attention.

"My father is buried in Arlington. How will we find his grave?"

"There is a directory at the administration building. What is his full name?

"PFC John Lee McDougal." Lee opened his envelope and took out a paper. "Here," he offered to Gertie. "The Army sent this to my mother about his burial."

Gertie studied the paper that had been well worn, opened and folded many times.

"Lee, your father was injured on June 7, 1944. Normandy."

"Yes, they brought him home to Walter Reed and he died there on July 29, 1944. Was buried on July 31, 1944."

Gertie went into deep thought. Should she ask if Lee's mother came to see his father at Walter Reed? Did she attend his funeral? She decided to give Lee time.

"Momma came here. I was two. I don't remember her going or coming back." He took a deep breath and continued.

"I learned when I was older that Momma visited Papa in the hospital. He seemed to be getting better..." he trailed off. "He died the day after Momma left him. She did not go to his funeral. Couldn't."

Lee turned to the window. Gertie let him have his time with difficult memories as they drove into the busy city. The approach to Arlington across the Memorial Bridge was awe-inspiring. Lee remained quiet.

"We're going to find Pa in all that?" He doubted as he saw thousands of headstones lined up the hill.

"Yes, we are," Gertie assured.

They found the gravestone for PFC John Lee McDougal. Lee sat down and embraced the stone. Gertie walked away to give Lee peace and time with his father. Was it fifteen minutes or twenty? She looked back and Lee had disappeared. Where was he? Gertie turned a full circle, and the boy was nowhere to be seen. She walked back to John McDougal's gravesite. Lee was not there. Did he wander off or did he run away? She walked back to the car very distressed that Lee would leave in such an unsettling way.

"We will wait for a while," she told the driver.

She was sharing the lunch basket with her driver when Lee suddenly appeared with tears streaming down his face.

"I don't know what to do. Where to go. I did what I came to do and then...."

The lost look on the young boy's face was beyond any terror Gertie had ever seen.

Lee reached out. "It was the only thing I wanted my whole life." His voice trembled as he stumbled forward. "Dad's not here. Not here," Lee spilled his anguish. "I thought I'd find something special to hold on to. My whole life. I wanted to find my father at Arlington." He stumbled and fell toward Gertie. "Can I go back to Hilltop? Please?" He was sobbing hysterically. His hands reached for Gertie. "Please. Take me back to Hilltop." By now he was doubled in half with pain and obviously suffering.

Gertie ran to him before he fell. "Of course, I will," she consoled and helped him in the car.

Lee took the fetal position, refused food and drink. He kept whispering, "Hilltop. Hilltop."

Gertie cleared the lunch and told the driver, "Let's go."

Chapter 6

PFC JOHN LEE McDOUGAL

The months and months of training were difficult—first in Maryland and then in Devon, England. It was difficult but the oversized, strong, young man did every task and made it look easy. Johnny knew what he was training for. He just did not know when it would happen. He became a leader as he exuded confidence in every physical challenge. Men wanted to be with or close to Johnny McDougal when the biggest test came on the shores of Normandy. On the fateful day, PFC John Lee McDougal donned his battle uniform, put a picture of Mary Ann and Lee in his helmet, loaded his gear, and got in the assigned line to board the transport boat. He was going to France.

The hardest part was still his need to see his family. Johnny was willing to do his duty, he was confident he could... even believed he would survive. He just wanted to see Mary Ann and see Lee before he landed on D-Day. Today more than ever. June 6th. Johnny wanted to meet his son. He was tired of waiting; he wanted to be launched into the war. He wanted to do what he had to do and go home.

PFC John McDougal boarded with his platoon and looked for his friend, PFC Phillip Gleason. Johnny had helped Phillip through all their training. He pushed in beside him and let his strength and undaunted spirit infuse the smallest, weakest soldier in his platoon. "We can do this, Phil," he assured. "Stay Close. I've got your back." The crossing was made in silence after those few words.

The landing on Normandy was measured in hours, not days. Johnny's platoon advanced. They had no idea if they were ahead of or behind the lines. The orders were clear and constantly shouted by the officers, "Move on! Move up!" They knew they had to move forward. It was terrifying. Rifles were not fired; they were so busy dodging enemy bullets and trying to find a place of cover in the next few yards. Machine gun blasts from the Germans' bunkers kept them pinned down. In the first uncounted hours, Johnny never got an enemy in the sights of his gun. They made slow progress across the sand, advancing when naval bombardments gave them room to move.

Johnny, Phillip, and six others dove into a slight trough near the base of the cement bunker and took a breath. In less than a second a German soldier appeared and with two shots wounded Phillip and killed another.

Instantly, Johnny knew they would all be killed. He rose up, brought his great bulk and ferocious anger before the German. In a split-second Johnny remembered Willy Klopik and before the German knew what this red-faced Goliath was doing, Johnny grabbed the hot barrel of the gun with his left hand and hit his enemy in the mouth with his powerful right fist. The rifle discharged into Johnny's leg. That did not stop the bully from Missouri. He disarmed the German and shot him. No doubt, without Johnny's actions all eight would have died there.

Although totally exposed to withering German fire, and

without concern for himself, PFC John L McDougal lifted Phillip onto his hip and led the scattered platoon up the hill to a place where they could do what they came on this beach to do. He dropped Phillip in a trench and stood on his battered leg to launch a hand grenade into a pillbox which was causing great damage to the still-landing troops up the dune behind them.

After the explosion, silence from the concrete bunker brought tears to Johnny's eyes.

When the medic came to help Phillip, Johnny realized he needed help, too. A bullet had entered his back at the waist. Adrenalin had masked the pain but now he twisted in anguish and passed out.

* * *

PFC John Lee McDougal woke up on a hospital stretcher six hours later. A medic whispered in his ear. "The war is over for you, soldier. You are one of the lucky ones. You are being transported back across the channel."

"My friend, Phillip…"

"He didn't make it."

Johnny was lucky that he did not die writhing in pain from his injuries on the sands of Normandy as many who could not be evacuated did. However, his injuries were extensive and critical. After his leg was amputated at the knee, he was sent to Walter Reed Hospital in Bethesda, Maryland, for his internal injuries. Mary Ann was notified.

Chapter 7

LEE

"Do you want to know why I came to Hilltop?" Lee asked Sunday evening as they sat on the porch eating dinner.

Gertie smiled and nodded. She knew he did not need any more coaching, Lee was ready to talk.

"My mother came to Maryland once. She said it was the second greatest day of her life after the day I was born. She came to see Dad at Walter Reed. I have it in a letter…"

Lee picked through his paper sack and finally found the letter he was looking for. It was not brown with age, nor did it appear to be worn from folding and unfolding. It looked crisp and new. It obviously was not written in 1944.

"My mother wrote to me." He offered the letter to Gertie.

Dearest Lee,

There are some things I want you to know about your father's service during the war. I am ashamed that I kept them to myself for so long. I have always felt that your father and his last chapters were too hard for you. It wasn't fair. Someday I was going to write the story for you, but I never did. I'm going to tell you everything before I die but I also need to write it down so you never forget.

If you are reading this letter, I am gone to be with Dad. We have already talked and you know the whole story. Attached to this letter is the story of our lives before you were born and the commendation for his medals. I hope it brings you comfort in the years ahead when you need to remember. I believe it will give you courage for the days ahead without me.

The box tied with a ribbon in my small chest has his medals. Among the service ribbons, there is the Congressional Medal of Honor—clearly marked for valor. It is the highest honor ever given and your father earned it. President Roosevelt personally presented it to him at Walter Reed Hospital.

You were two years old when I went to see your father in the hospital. We both knew it was our last time together. We sat in the ugly hospital room and held hands for the whole first day. The second day, something magical happened. A team of USO volunteers arrived and got permission to take him (and me) out of the hospital for two days. A nurse was assigned. The three of us were transported to Hilltop USO near Laurel, Maryland.

From the white and harsh hospital room to a lovely country estate. Rolling hills, apple orchards, stables of beautiful horses, cool country breezes, lively and friendly people. The woman who ran the USO greeted us as if she had been waiting for us and we were the only guests she had. Her name is Gertie Morgan. She was our angel, and it was magical.

At Hilltop, I found again the Johnny McDougal that I love. I had missed him for so long and he wasn't at Walter Reed. His smile, personality and remaining life were at Hilltop. We could relax and hold hands without clutching them against the future. Every time he opened his eyes, he saw me with a backdrop of beauty. I'm not sure you understand because you have never seen Hilltop. The joy we needed, one more time, was at Hilltop. He was tired and slept a lot. Always short naps. Your father did not want to sleep away the time we had and the time at Hilltop. Sometimes on the veranda overlooking the orchard, heavy with apples. Sometimes in the great room listening to music. Sometimes in the private room set up for us for two nights. Sometimes after one bite of apple pie. Always together and believing we had some time before facing the hard truth. I truly believe, if we had not gone to Hilltop, I would never have really found your father again. He was at Hilltop, and I was, too. We could say goodbye.

Gertie could not find words as she gently folded the letter for Lee to put back in his little sack.

"I have all the letters my mother saved about Hilltop USO. Dad wrote them while he was here. They have Laurel, Maryland postmarks." He opened the bag so Gertie could see the several letters inside. "I know the orchard and stables. I know the library and the porches. I know about the apple pies." Lee got more excited. "My father helped to harvest the apples that fall. It is all as Dad wrote in his letters." Lee paused in the longest spiel he had said since he arrived yesterday.

Just as Gertie was about to speak, Lee began again.

"I knew the big door and sat leaning against it. It was like the cover of a book that had a wonderful story inside. It came open and I fell inside." Lee's eyes were lit with joy; his countenance was beaming. "I knew Gertie Morgan would take me to Arlington. Just knew it!"

"I wanted to see my father's grave and read the stone. I wanted to find my Dad, but Dad was not there. I knew it right away. I was at Arlington Cemetery and the stone said *PFC John Lee McDougal,* but he was not there." Lee looked up at Gertie as he remembered how lost he was at Arlington. "It is a beautiful place full of honor… but just like Mom, I had to come to Hilltop to find my Dad. He is here." His hand flew in a circle around his head. "Here, at Hilltop."

Gertie will remember for the rest of her life Lee's face sprinkled with freckles, tears flowing down from his eyes across the freckles, and cheeks to the broadest, happiest smile ever captured on a young boy's face. All the while repeating, "Hilltop. Hilltop."

* * *

Lee found a home and family at Hilltop and never went back to Missouri. Gertie became his grandmother. He let Maggie boss him around and Bertha cook his meals. Sam Jr. taught him to ride a horse, tend the stable, and became his best friend.

Often in the evenings, Lee went to the bench in the orchard to commune with his mother. Mary Ann was always there. And standing back under an apple tree, Big Johnny McDougal gave Lee his attention.

Attention is all a boy needs from his father.

The End

* * *

Epilog

Lee graduated from Laurel Junior/Senior High School and the University of Maryland. Gertie gave Lee his first typewriter—a Royal 1955 model with magic margins. He began writing and never stopped. His genre was nonfiction. His book, *Gertie* (published in 2014) under the pen name, Faye Green, tells the full story of Gertie MacGregor Morgan and Hilltop Manor.

Bertha's Apple Pie

Prepare Apples

Peel, core and slice 8 apples—enough to fill the pie plate and pile high. Don't slice too thin or too thick. Place in a bowl and drizzle with 2 Tbs molasses.
Blend
1 cup sugar
1 tsp cinnamon
Dash Nutmeg
2½ Tbs flour
¼ tsp salt
Toss sugar mixture over apples. Stir several times in the next 30 minutes while making the crust. Set aside.

Crust

⅔ cup of chilled lard
2 cups flour
1 tsp salt
2 Tbs sugar
Blend dry ingredients in a large bowl. Cut lard in using two knives working quickly until it is in pea size pieces

½ cup iced water sprinkled over. Pull together with a fork until a soft ball. Divide in two and save half for the lattice top. Roll the other half on a floured board until it fits a 10-inch glass pie plate. Crimp the edge.

Assembly

Fill the pie crust with the apples. Dot with 2 Tbs Butter cut into small pieces. Drizzle with 2 Tbs fresh lemon juice. Set in ice box while you make the lattice for the top.

Roll the remaining half of pie crust on a floured board. Cut into ¾ inch strips. Weave the lattice pie crust strips acors the pie and pinch the edges into the crimped edge of the bottom crust. Brush with a small amount of milk ;and sprinkle with cinnamon sugar.

Bake

Bake in preheated, 350 degree oven for 45 – 50 minutes. Pie needs to be bubbling up and golden brown. Time varies according to the apples.

Bertha's Advice: put a tray under it or it will "bubbly over and mess your stove."

Arlington

Suddenly, at that moment, the sun went behind a cloud
The wind blew sharply, and flags rose to attention.

The soft brown wood caught the light
The horse stood quietly upright
The Red, the White and the Blue bound
The life of service gone down.

Soft cadence was called in a muffled tone
Each walked without him, feeling alone
Among the homes of many who served
Where every marker looked the same
Except on close look where it is carved
A different state; a different name.

They lifted the flag above the box
The sun finally found a way
To make fifty stars a stencil
On the box, the heart, the day.

The volley of gunfire shook the scene
Expected but the decibels mean
The bugle sent the soldier to rest
A folded flag, perfection at its best
Was handed with the expression
"You have the thanks of a Grateful Nation."

A man who knows his place in life
Believes in freedom and sacrifice
Who knows love of God and family
Are wrapped up in his country's need
He is sure and safe in heaven's care
Because he stood - right there.

Grandma Poe

There are many stories I could write about my grand-mother, Minnie Poe. She lived to age 97 and the story I've decided to tell happened very late in her life. Grandma was a small, spunky lady who had met many challenges during her life. At her 88th birthday, she proclaimed her age and weight were now the same. She was tiny and her 5-foot frame had shrunk until the youngest grandchild looked her straight in the eye. Her white hair was always secured in a bun at the nape of her head and she had several flowered house dresses to complete her look. Grandma's domain was 203 Tenth Street, Laurel, Maryland. She swept the walk daily, even the curb. She loved to walk, never owned a car or learned to drive one. Grandma often strode down Tenth, right on Montgomery Street; right on Eleventh Street; right on Patuxent Road back to Tenth. Her 'perfect square' as she liked to call it. Often when stopping to visit Grandma, it would be necessary to sit on the porch and wait for her coming around the corner ... or else strike out around the block to meet and walk back home with her.

This story begins on a sunny, warm day when Grandma took her walk...

At the corner of Eleventh Street, she decided to turn left and go two blocks north and visit Ivy Hill Cemetery. It could be that she had done this many times before—no one knows. But this day became one our family talked about for years.

At the cemetery, Grandma wandered to read the markers on the families she knew. Poe. Beall. Stanton. Spread out in the far corners. It was a great day to be outside and she had the energy to walk and when she needed to sit, there were memorial benches. Soon it was time to go back to Tenth Street. However she was turned around and left the cemetery at the wrong exit. Eleventh Street was not straight ahead. Several homes she passed were recognized, but they were not on the way home. Soon the sidewalk ended, and her path was not clear. The shoulder of the road was not without challenges. Stones and pebbles were difficult. Fatigue began to weigh on Minnie Poe and she knew she was not close to home. Was she on Brooklyn Bridge Road or Sandy Spring Road? Not sure. Finally, she had to rest so she moved off the shoulder to sit on a clear place—her knees pulled up and her dressed tucked around—her arms wrapping her knees to hold it all together.

How would this story end for my grandmother, ninety plus years? Tired, alone and lost?

That same afternoon, Naomi Hufmann was finishing her housework when a honking horn in her driveway got her attention. I'm not expecting a package from UPS, she thought as she went out to greet the driver.

"I have special delivery for Naomi Hufmann," he said as he turned back to his van and extended his hand.

Nothing could have surprised Naomi Hufmann more than Minnie Poe stepping lightly out of the UPS truck.

"She asked me if I knew where Gilbert and Naomi Hufmann lived? The little lady said she could walk home from there. So, here we are."

Grandma greeted Naomi with a broad grin as she pointed past the Hufmann yard to the nearest Ivy Hill exit and straight down Eleventh Street. She was not lost any more.

"Sit right here on the lawn chair Mrs. Poe, while I bring my car from the garage. I'm taking you to Tenth Street."

From that day on, Naomi loved to tell the story about the day Grandma was delivered by United Parcel Service. The family is forever grateful that the UPS driver stopped to help the little lady sitting by the side of the road.

Grandma never mentioned it.

The End

Note: In the telling of this story, we were often asked if we officially thanked the driver or told UPS of his kindness. No. He could have lost his job for taking a passenger in his van. We hope he felt rewarded knowing he helped a sweet lady in need.

Arizona has beckoned many times. The beautiful cities, the red rocks of Sedona, the native American culture, and the glorious Grand Canyon are known to many. In 2013, the unique opportunity to drive an ATV up the mountains to the high desert provided a true immersion in an Arizona experience. Not many Delaware ladies can say, "I did that!"

The High Desert, Arizona

The sun lit the east side of the mountains. The saguaro cacti guarded every slope and stood sentry on every pinnacle. The sky brightened in the morning and painted itself deep blue. The desert mountains begged to be disturbed by the roar of ATV machines made for this adventure.

The roadside signs were graphic pictures of four-wheel drive vehicles. They warned that you would need a special vehicle and the road ahead was 'primitive'.

Today's adventure was the Arizona mountains, a deep valley, and high desert. The well- paved road was misleading as it ended abruptly and dared you to continue on a well-worn path of red dirt. I looked down the primitive road and I knew that I would have to eventually go up and over, down and around the mountains that impressed me in every direction.

I wrapped myself in a warm jacket and pulled on gloves against the temps that were to climb to near 60 degrees but had not broken 50 yet.

A rugged trail machine was backed off the trailer. Emblazoned across the bumper and door—Rhino. I had never been close to a rhinoceros, or a machine named for one. It seemed appropriate for the road ahead.

The experienced leader gave minimal instructions.

Turn the key to start

 Two pedals—one to go—one to stop

 If you need to back up, drop into reverse

Follow me and keep up.

Never relax your grip on the wheel.

It was going to be a day of testing for the woman from Delaware, where flat farmland only goes in one direction—a few feet down to sea level. This is a long, long way from home.

The entry road was surprisingly smooth, with a few bumps and some small rocks about the size of a loaf of bread. The secured seat belt and half wind shield gave a feeling of security. The accelerator gave just the right thrust and the steering wheel fit my small hands. The lead vehicle stayed 20 feet ahead. Another followed 20 feet behind. The animal vehicle began to feel comfortable, even when a wash or two bumped a bit higher and swerved a bit hard to the right or left. It was beginning to be fun.

My eyes were on the road, but I relaxed enough to admire the amazing landscapes moving by, close to the open vehicle and slowly on the far horizon. Arizona is ever-changing. The eternal mountains and ancient cacti are filtered in light that changes perceptions and perspective. Snow fell this week and some of the higher peaks were white. Those white peaks back-dropped high colors—orange, red, gold, amber, crimson, pink, purple—that had not been noticed before. A long mesa spread along the horizon was blackened by the shadow of the rising sun. Eastern cliffs, dripping sheer rock, glowed in morning sun. The mesa was enchanting. If only I could go there and run along the flat top. Becoming overconfident, no doubt.

The further we went the less smooth the road, although still red and well worn. There were canyons to look into—deep drops off to the left and to the right. It was important to keep an eye to the roadbed. A pie-shaped wash, cut into the roadside made by rain washing down the mountainside, could snag a wheel and lead to disaster. The caravan stopped so the dangers could be reiterated to the novice. An unplanned tumble could cause a meeting with a rock much larger than a loaf of bread, or an unyielding cactus with thousands of weapons always pointing, or worse—death. It was time to focus seriously.

The terrain and the Rhino became instructors. At times, motion through the desert became more important than the scenery. It had something to do with the feeling of being one with the Rhino. Tension melted away and driving was part of the enjoyment. In some stretches our caravan increased speed, accelerated on slight inclines, and hopped over the less intimidating crests. Airborne. Whee!

Across a small valley, not even a valley, maybe a breath between mountains, a huge grove of palm trees appeared. High above any other vegetation very tall palm trees, with years of brown downward-turned palms below a vibrant green crown of palms, reached for the sun. An oasis in the middle of the desert mountain. Suddenly it was there! Beautiful, absolutely mesmerizing. Its contrast to the desert around was astounding. Green grass carpeted the flat floor circled by the palms. The sound of water was musical; magical. Somewhere in the midst of this oasis there was a bubbling hot spring. It was luxury for the eyes. As with all oases, by their very nature, travelers want to stay. It spoke relief and recess from the dust and challenging road. But alas, there were restrictions—a high fence and no admittance signs We could not go to the waters. We e stood in the shade on the grass and stored the vision. The oasis' restorative power cannot translate into words, but it is felt.

It was time to move on.

A sign told me the road ahead would be 'Dangerous. Experienced Drivers Only'. I read the notice with a smile and noted that I had 90 minutes of experience. Our leader stopped us for a moment and reminded us to hold tight to the steering wheel. The danger here was not falling into an abyss; it was losing control and tipping over. The leader's lesson and warnings were clear.

"Let's go! Keep up!"

We entered a dry riverbed. A sign warned me not to cross if there was water present. No chance; no risk. Not a sign of water. The bed was dry, sunbaked rocks and sand. Some places were soft-shifting sand; some were rocky gravel lanes. Everywhere there was evidence of rushing, raging, flooding waters but always in some distant time. The riverbed shouted dry, answering the loud noise from my raging Rhino. Rocks and sand pulled the wheels. The steering wheel challenged my grip. We were far from the even red road of a few miles back. Desert brush reached from the riverbank and pulled on my jacket and left burrs. All streams, dry or rushing for eons, have been slicing between mountains creating deep canyons, and this one was no different. Soon steep walls of stone boxed our views. They were close and echoed the loud Rhino roars.

Suddenly, the river offered wide vistas over flat plains which lacked urgency of motion witnessed in the canyon. Almost quiet to my ringing ears.

Amazingly, new signs announced Private Property and the most remote homes imaginable dotted the landscape. Could this road be someone's driveway? Maybe they come in from different, less challenging ways. I learned as I drove on and on….either way…this rocky twisted unpredictable road was the driveway for maybe twenty homes scattered in these mountains and canyons along the riverbed.

It takes a lot of strength to hold the steering wheel when

the road (or lack thereof) gives the front wheel a mind of its own. Once on a rocky ledge the steering wheel spun out of my hands. I grabbed and held by unknown strength. Tired fingers, tense grip. Hands aching and still strong. The road is held. Control is maintained. It is not just the scenery, the discovery of remote places, and fun with friends. It was discovery! The driver has learned a lot about herself. The Rhino is tamed. The sheer joy and mastery of the high desert exhilarates.

A sharp left turn leaves the riverbed and leads to untracked places. Now we are really off-road. There is absolutely nothing predictable here. No tire tracks. No signs telling what's ahead. It could be that no one has ever turned down this space between these scattered cacti before. There are rocks, ledges, and small cliffs. More instruction:

Take the incline straight. Push straight up.

Accelerate.

Decline straight down.

Ease up on the gas.

The jarring and jousting is constant. Laughing is spontaneous. It is a nervous laugh, but no one can hear over the roar of the Rhino. No fear—admiration for the vehicle that is eating the mountain for me. Over one, two, three small cliffs. Soon the caravan reenters the trail after an exciting roller coaster ride before ending the day. The leader is smiling. He knows I could not have done this trail hours ago. But now, yes. I can leap small cliffs . . and love it.

What I saw, the fears I conquered, the driving I mastered, the oasis I found, the memories I hold, the beauty and the respect I acquired for the high desert mountains, are my unique Arizona experience.

Faye

Dedicated to the Lynn and Del Taylor families
of Arizona and Utah

Fiona

The man I was forced to marry when I was thirteen, just died. Here by the window, I am drinking tea and waiting for the undertaker. It has been quite a journey.

I recall....

CHAPTER 1

I was just a girl—tiny and scared when they took me away.

I remember the day like it was yesterday. The Matron awakened me early and took me to the barber room to get my hair cut. They made me take a bath and it wasn't my haircut or bath day. The clothes they gave me were the same drab dress and cover apron, but they were clean, and it was not the day for clean clothes. The Matron inspected my shoes, and decided my soft-sole issue shoes were fine. In a small room beyond the dining hall, four tiny, scared girls were trying to swallow. A glass of milk sat by my plate, and it was not Wednesday. A cloth bag was pushed into my hand. I let it drop. They pushed it back in my hand and I began to cry. I knew something different was happening to me in this place of sameness and I was scared.

It was Arabella who told me. "We be leaving the workhouse."

"Leaving?"

"Leaving forever," she replied.

How could I be leaving? My family is here. Ma. Da. Patrick. Sean. Mavis. I have school today. My brain kept questioning—leaving? I was so far into denial that I could not ask the obvious—where we be goin'?

I ate the food and drank the milk as I looked at the other girls, freshly trimmed, bathed, and dressed, each eating their portion and each with a cloth bag on the floor beside their chair. I knew Arabella. We sat next to each other in school and tried to do our work details together. The others were just faces that I had seen.

Tears made my milk salty; there were so many. Trembling shoulders and quivering mouth were allowed as long as I did not sob or make a sound. The Matron did not like crying girls. A year living in the workhouse had taught me.

When I had my thirteenth birthday, The Matron greeted me as she did each girl. "You are a woman now. Stop acting like a child." On the day when I had my first menstrual period, The Matron had another announcement as she handed me a pouch with rag squares. "Keep yourself clean, woman." That was three weeks after my birthday. Now, two months into my adulthood, Arabella tells me we are leaving the workhouse.

The Matron rapped the table. "On your feet. Get your bag. Follow me." She led us out across the large empty exercise yard. No one was to see us go. How many days did I hope to see Ma, Patrick, or Da in this yard? I trailed slowly behind, and I stopped not-believing—I was leaving Portumna, and I knew—my family did not know. I was about to be gone.

At the last minute before entering the building across the square, I looked back and up. The sun lit the window on the second floor. Patrick was in the window! Patrick saw me. Patrick knew. Patrick would come for me. He would make this right. I would not melt into nothing. Patrick would save me.

I waved, blew a kiss, and entered the door to the Administration Building which closed with a loud prophetic clunk.

The Matron spoke to each as we climbed into the waiting carriage. "Forget Portumna. Forget your family." My river of tears stopped. I wondered if that was her last mean slash, or would there be more where she was taking us.

Arabella and I sat together in the carriage, holding hands tightly, not daring to enjoy the ride or even our friendship. We were not allowed to enjoy anything, and we knew not to talk.

Four young ladies and a chaperone, with picnic sandwiches in our bag, riding in a carriage for the first time in our lives, across the beautiful Erin Isle countryside, on a perfect June morning—not able to enjoy any of it. Too frightened, almost petrified with fear. Grieving for our families.

CHAPTER 2

I tried to remember each village we passed hoping to know my way back to Ma. My mind was exhausted working on this puzzle. Sleep overtook me and I napped to the rumble of the wagon wheels. The Matron woke me up with her announcement. "Sligo."

It was a mistake to believe I had reached my destination. The Matron called, "Sarah. Kathleen. Mary." Three girls picked up their bags, climbed out of the carriage and were rushed out of sight. Arabella held tight to my hand. I could feel her trembling, as was I. The Matron climbed back in the carriage and directed the driver, "Proceed." The carriage jerked to motion and continued moving with me, Arabella, our fears, and The Matron.

In a short time, we stopped again at a waterfront. The ships anchored there were the biggest things I had ever seen, bobbing against the docks. "Get your bags. Get out. We are here." They were the last words I heard from The Matron. The sights, sounds and smells aroused a fear so strong that I felt sick and wanted to die. Can I die? Can I make myself die?

The Matron reached for me. I drew back and her hand missed my arm and got Arabella. With an evil glance at me, the Matron pulled Arabella from the carriage and delivered her to a man waiting. I saw Arabella half running half stumbling trying to keep up with her arm—being pulled by her escort—moving ever away from me. Arabella's eyes, looking back, were pleading, do something. I could not help her; I could not help myself. I was delivered in the same way to another escort. I looked again at the empty cobblestone path where last I saw her. "Arabella," I cried. Goodbye, Arabella. Goodbye.

Water, wind, and sea spray assaulted my eyes as I tried to take in the scene. Huge ships rocked and banged the dock. People were bustling all around. The escort was pulling, almost dragging me. Suddenly, I could not breathe. My chest constricted and a chill made my head crawl. Trembling shook my body, and I could not hold my sack. I thought, The Matron will be angry, before the earth began to move like the sea. The sky went under me; the earth rose over my head. I fell down but floated up. Black calm kept me from dying.

When I came to, The Matron was nowhere. I was on a palette in a dark corner of a slowly swaying cave. I tried to sit up and banged my head.

"Roll out before ye sit up," a voice advised. "I think it be better to stay put for a bit," it continued.

Fear overtook me and I began to cry again as I turned my back to the voice.

"I know ye be scared. Me, too. I be on this ship two days, rockin' and goin' nowhere. Me already decided…tears no good….fear worse. There be twelve girls like us. Each day, two, three more. All from workhouses. Ye be from a workhouse?"

"Aye, Portumna," I answered turning back to face the voice.

"Molly Sullivan," she introduced.

"Fiona. Fiona Doyle," I replied in a whisper, and again turned my back to her.

Immediately, I regretted giving my name. I missed Arabella and did not want another friend. My anguish was beyond pain. My arm hurt. My head, aching. My knees, torn and bloody. And I did not want conversation. Molly Sullivan had the gift of gab and began to talk, ignoring my resistance.

"We be goin' somewhere but not knowin' where. Why else on a ship? Here we sit bobbin' up and down. Waitin' to go. Ye hasn't walked on this thing yet. Take care. The floor ever movin' under foot. It be a good idea for you to try to walk, me thinks before the boat really moves. 'Tis strange feelin'." She took a breath before changing the subject.

"We get fed once each day. Chamber pots in far corner. The pots be nasty already. Careful nothing splashes on ye dress. That be awful smell to come back to ye bed for a trip. Me hopes the trip not be long. They tells me when I be brought here that we get a short time up top for fresh air each day but that donno' start till we be moving. Fiona Doyle, we be goin' on a sea voyage."

"Could we be goin' to England?" I speculated, still looking at the black wall behind my bed.

"Nay, we leavin the west coast of Ireland. England be east.

That be me figurin'," Molly surmised. "We goin' west."

'What be west," I asked, unable to recall a geography lesson. "West?" I asked again. Now my stomach was bobbing like the ship and my brain bobbed too, as Molly Sullivan continued talking.

"Sit up, Fiona. It better sitting up. Stomach tryin' to get right-side. Ye gotta git up. Walk. No matter how hard. Me learned the first day. Falling down, bad. Hard gettin' back up."

Sitting up did help. My stomach became more agreeable. I looked at Molly for the first time and noticed she was bigger and older than me. A rough carved cane was propped against her bed. One small foot peeked from her folded legs opposite a full-sized foot. She had a bobbed head of dark hair above a generous smiling mouth. Two beautiful lash-laced eyes stared honestly at me. In spite of the circumstance, I warmed to Molly Sullivan.

"When we eat, save some in ye pocket. The empty stomach later be worse." Molly reached into her pocket to show a crust of brown bread. "Ye missed today's feeding, Fiona. Open ye sack, there be supper, of some sort. Ye feel better."

I ate from my sack but did not abandon my question. "What be west?"

"Ocean. Wide ocean. Atlantic. When we moving, the rising sun behind us; the setting sun, ahead. Me be checking as soon as we begin." She took a breath. "It's called the deck."

"The deck?"

"Aye, when ye go up top for fresh air, ye be standing on the deck. This place where we sleep called below. They tell us 'to the deck' or 'go below'. Move quickly or a push comes to ye. 'Tis a man, no matron. He tell us what to do and fetch our meal."

"Does he frighten ye?" I needed to know where my fear would go.

"Nay, old and harmless." Molly's face reflected humor. "The Old Man be wanting us to move along and gets onery at slow moving girls. Needs to get back to his rum and cigar. Mostly irritated by us." She smiled, "I'm the pokey one," and patted her cane.

The ship tossed and the dim light made shadows with each movement. My bed was hard and musty. My fear turned into a manageable fright. The girl looking back at me was a shining light. I needed a friend, so I resisted the impulse to throw my face into my bed and bawl. It was easier, even smarter to respond to the ray of hope curled up in the next bunk. Molly did not especially select me, and she was not chosen by me. I just happened to be the girl tossed, unconscious in the bed next to hers. Providence.

"Fiona, use my name so we be friends—Molly."

"Molly."

"Fiona and Molly," she smiled a smile that went into me.

CHAPTER 3

After my ability to walk on the ever-moving floor was proven, I began a study of everything around me. Light came down from the opening to the deck and four very small openings on each side near the ceiling. There were no candles or lanterns. Fortunately, the days are long, and night—only a few hours. I did not care the time, but I wanted to count the days that I traveled away from my family and the days before Patrick would come for me. I reached to the wall above my head and scratched the first day-line with my fingernail.

Identical pallets lined the wall. A rough woven blanket finished the bed. The open space in the middle was slightly bigger than the table centered and bolted to the floor. No chairs in the space. I surmised we would eat standing at the table. We were allowed to move about below but I did not feel comfort on the ever moving vessel.

Sixteen girls filled the pallets along the walls. Ribs of the vessel divided the pallets into pairs. Molly was the oldest of all the girls quartered with us. Most of the girls were quiet. My bed was not near the loud exceptions. Molly and I had our space. Fear and apprehension kept me from reaching out to others, and surely, they felt the same. I was content to stay on my pallet and be quiet.

There were a lot of questions I wanted to ask Molly. She was a riddle, being so different from the other girls.... and so smart. Was it her age? Will I be wiser in a couple more years? I did not have to ask my questions, Molly loved to talk.

"I be sixteen in two months. How old?" she asked me.

"Just made thirteen."

"Me managed to avoid this," she threw her arm in a circle, " twice. When I knew girls were being sent out of the work-house, I got sick. Made meself have dysentery. The Matron never put that problem on a ship," she laughed.

My silence and big eyes invited her to go on.

Molly lay back on the bed with her story, not wanting her words to go further. "Aye, I ate rhubarb root, yucky and sour, to keep me off the list. It was a nasty choice, but I had to think of Beatrice. She be my sister and the last of my family. No leave her. So, the night before the girls were lined up to go, wit their sacks and hearty breakfast, Molly Sullivan be in the la-trine. The Matron came to make sure it was not a faking. Glory be. She nearly passed out at the sight and smell. Molly Sullivan be off the list, stayed behind and missed the sailing twice." The thought of it brought a giggle into the story.

"What happened this time, Molly? No rhubarb?"

"There be rhubarb aplenty at the corner of the building. Still there for the wanting. This year, me be ready to go. It be me own choice." Molly's countenance changed. "Beatrice died. She be the last."

"So sorry. So sorry," I offered.

Molly smiled and continued. "Me choice be stay in the workhouse or go see what can be meant for Molly in the world. Me asked God and He said, go. Here I be. No rhubarb root this year. Me own choice to come wit hope…. and, to be ye friend, Fiona"

Molly seemed worn out by the telling and got quiet with her thoughts. After a moment, she took charge again. "Go to the pot, Fiona. Then be my turn. We be taking refuge in sleep now."

Before exhaustion took me to sleep, Molly spoke again.

"No telling what be ahead for ye and me, Fiona. But we know how hard the workhouse be. We need to have faith that what be ahead, be better."

I agreed with my silence, but I had more fear than Molly. So, I said to myself, so I could sleep—Patrick will come for me. He promised.

CHAPTER 4

The next day we were awakened by noises that told something was changing. Banging and shouting. Rushing and cursing. The words coming down from the deck were: Rope! Grab! Throw! Tie! Mainsail! Jib! Tide! All with great urgency. Suddenly, for a minute, a hush pervaded, and the swaying universe moved precisely in one direction before loud activity resumed on deck. We had left the dock on the early morning tide.

"Me thinks we have left Ireland," I whispered.

"Sure'en we have," Molly agreed

I reached up and scratched my second day-line on the wall and dropped back into my nest.

"Are ye goin' to cry again, Fiona? Would be wasted tears. Me suggest ye save em' for some future cause. Come, girl. Tell me about ye family."

It was a good distraction to the realization that I was leaving my homeland. "The Doyle cottage be north of Galway till the potato died. Ma, Da, Patrick, Sean, and Mavis. And me makes six into Portumna workhouse. Rumors in Portumna say Sean ran away. Now me be on a ship in the ocean only four left. I not be seeing them from the day we went in. Did ye know that how it be?"

Molly shook her head in agreement.

"Patrick my big brother." Fiona choked, thinking of Patrick. "He promised to look after me in the workhouse, but he never saw me again until the day me left. Patrick be keeping his promise to me. Across the ocean if need be."

"The ocean wide," Molly reminded.

"Patrick's promise—bigger."

"You keep that thought, my friend. It be helpin' ye. Maybe me needs to think of something to keep me on dark days." Molly went quiet with this thought.

"I donno' know how but something deep inside tells that Patrick will find me. Even more than my hope to see Ma again. A mystery because me love and miss me Ma terribly." I was absolutely positive. "Patrick be comin'."

"Ye have me convinced. Maybe me be meetin' Patrick Doyle someday." She smiled. "We movin'. This be a good time to eat a bit of the bread we saved back. Think of ye stomach."

"Tell ye story, Molly," I urged.

"The Sullivan's cottage be near Carrick-on-Shannon. The potato died, as did me Pa, me brother Dennis and Baby Mary. Ma said no more dying, so we go in. Ma, Beatrice and Molly, She knew we be separated but her girls would be together. Beatrice and me see each other because we near the same age.

Sometimes at work or in yard. The Matron caution us if'n we linger together. Ma died. Beatrice died. Now, only me. The workhouse holds no more of this Sullivan family. Me leavin' none behind."

She looked over with compassion to her new friend. "It be harder for ye, Fiona." Molly really did understand.

After a quiet time of getting used to the new movement of the ship, The Old Man announced, "Dinner."

"Must be noon," Molly said. She got up and took her cane. It was the first time I could view her difficulty in full light. The small left foot supported her weight well, but it was obvious her left leg was shorter. The tall, beautiful girl walked with a slight side-to-side rock on an ever-moving floor. The rhythmic tap of the cane accompanied her. She still managed a strong demeaner and walked with her head high. Molly looked back at me and smiled as if to say, comin?'

Life settled in on the rocking vessel. It was always moving and swaying—sometimes more than others. Molly and I shared all our stories, hopes, and dreams. Our fears and insecurities. When the water and wind were wild, we clung and rolled together on one pallet. In the big storm, many day-lines out, we prayed for deliverance. Water washed in the openings near the ceiling.

"Quick," Molly directed. "Put your pallet over mine. We can keep one dry." From then on, we slept together on the dry pallet. Nothing that gets soaked ever completely dries below. After the storm, heat, and humidity, unlike any we had ever known, assaulted us. We were always thirsty. The allotment of drinking water was not enough.

A fine white film began to show on our skin. "Salt," Molly said. "Taste it, Fiona. Salt. Even the water we get to wash with is salty. 'Tis better not to wash."

Molly and I walked the deck and discussed the immense

sea. We Irish girls became seasoned sailors—assessing the ever-changing conditions and working as a team on the problems of living on an ocean vessel. Fortunately, neither of us suffered the sea sickness that plagued many other girls. We counted the days and wondered where we were going. And we never admitted to each other that we would eventually be separated but each, in her own mind, knew.

On a rainy day, we took off our shoes and cover-apron to stand in the renewing water from heaven. The salt was washed away. We stood most of the next two days letting our clothes dry out and slept on the already damp pallet that we pulled from underneath. Damp and salt were enemies but together we managed better than most of the girls. Several days later, Molly and I slept dry and unsalted before the ever-present humidity, dampness and salt assaulted again.

It seemed we had talked of everything when a question came to my mind. "Molly, how did ye know ye be on a list to leave? I be wondering. That morning a surprise to me."

"Aye, 'tis a surprise to all, 'cept me. 'Tis a secret, me can tell ye." Molly lowered her voice and leaned closer. "Readin'. Ye friend Molly can read. I be workin' cleanin' the office and readin' all that lay around. Ma began teachin' when I be four years old. That a good thing because the workhouse stops schoolin' at twelve years."

"True. My schoolin' at Portumna ended a month after arrivin'. Schooling was the best part, but I had only it a short while. Ma taught the alphabet and writing me own name, but babies come and hard times. Me forgetting her lessons except Fiona Doyle. Can still write that."

"I can read anything and even talk in the English-way but I choose not to."

"Why?" I asked, wanting to hear her story.

Molly settled down on her bed, set her cane aside. She was

about to tell a story.

"Fiona, if I talk in the English-way, they know I can read. Reading is a skill. Keeping it a secret makes it an advantage. If The Matron knows I read, I be watched more and not allowed in place where it be useful. So, I decided to keep it a secret and talk in the cottage-way." She paused and changed her language. "I got a job cleaning the Administration building. Then my secret became valuable. I read about girls being sent away and Molly Sullivan was on the list. My secret kept me from being sent away while Beatrice lives." Molly's eyes closed on the memory of her dead sister. She dropped back on her bed.

I lay back on my bed, astounded at Molly's story. Sleep was drifting on me when Molly continued using her old language style.

"Aye, Fiona, readin' important secret. Very useful when all around, ye be thought ignorant. The list to Canada and Australia. Listen girl, I be tellin'. If'n we dock in 40 days, we be in Canada. If'n we still be rockin' in this boat after ye makes 40 day-lines on the wall, we be going to Australia—halfway round the world. It be written and I be readin'."

My heart leapt in my chest. How will Patrick get to Australia? Dear God, not Australia, I prayed.

"Me thinks we be goin' to Canada. The sun be ever before us when we go to the deck. That be the best sign."

I took comfort in Molly's last words and thanked God. I had to believe He would not want me to go to Australia.

"Ye and me be lost sheep praying for deliverance. Praying that the rest of our lives not be so hard. 'Tis not too much to ask of God."

We fell silent in the realities that overwhelmed us. The vessel ever-moving. The ocean, so wide. Thirst nagging. Salt drying. Skin itching. Mouth sore. Eyes dry. Alone, except for each other. Just before taking refuge in asleep, I gave Molly my last thought of the day.

"Can ye teach me to read, Molly?"

"Aye, I can."

CHAPTER 5

"Fiona, we begin the teachin' today."

Molly reached into her bag and took out a pamphlet—well-worn, weakened on the folds, and soiled. "This be the English Union rules on feeding at the workhouse. I took it to practice readin' time ago. No one noticed it gone. Fiona, it be very tirin' to read about mealtime and food lists over and over but all I have for readin' for a year or more. That last morning, I put it in my undies and brought it with me. 'Twill be useful for me practicin' and Fiona learnin'." Molly became pensive. "All along, I wished I had a Bible like Ma taught."

Molly started her teaching; I was an attentive student. She insisted that I correct my speech at the same time. It became easy to use the correct verbs during our reading sessions and go back to the cottage way when on deck or mealtime with the other girls. We did alphabet work on the dirty floor behind the pallet—erasing and rewriting according to the lesson. Molly loved to teach. I loved to learn. Soon I was reading the food list easily and mastering the sentences.

Day after day. Every day. Teacher and student were immersed in the only written words available to us. Soon, I recited the whole pamphlet. Twenty-two day-lines were scratched on my wall.

"Fiona, think of the letters and sounds you have learned. There are so many words you want to know that aren't in this dirty old pamphlet. Mother, father, love, sunset, sad, happy, Jesus, to name a few. The names of your brothers and sister. Now, imagine how a word looks. Picture the letters for the sounds and try to write it in the dust."

Molly was a natural teacher. She wanted me to read not memorize. I was a good student. This exercise became the highlight of my day. Each day I had new words to spell, sound, and claim. I wanted to be able to read the Bible someday, too. We both longed for books—something of more substance than the Union pamphlet reminding us constantly of the workhouse.

"Molly, we will have a Bible someday. I have faith." I proclaimed with surety. "I will read the Bible."

That day was burned in my memory. It was the day that reading gave me confidence in myself. Gave me hope. Could it be that learning to read made the salt, mustiness, constant motion, poor food, and even the unknown, less intimidating to me?

Each day the girls below got fed at noon. Then we got time up on a part of the deck set aside for us. Molly and I did not know that we were cargo. While other passengers traveled without pallets, regular meals and time on deck, the girls below fared better. We thought the damp, salty days were difficult, but did not know that twice below, in the belly of the ship, other passengers were starving, sharing disease, and dying. Still the long journey was taking a toll on all the girls, including Molly and me. Boredom, inactivity, lack of water, and spoiled food made us lethargic. Often, we fell asleep in the middle of a lesson. Only the Old Man's food call gave us the time of day. The hours blended. Boredom worsened with the dirty and worn pamphlet. It became hard to repeat and repeat my lesson and impossible to concentrate.

Thirty-two day-lines were scratched on the wall when I admitted to myself, and to Molly, that I was sick. Everything hurt. My body. My head. My eyes. I could not eat the stale bread and gruel that the Old Man brought.

"No lessons, today, Molly."

"Take ye bread, Fiona. Ye canno' roll on this boat wit empty stomach. Ye not gonna di. Me promise ye. Me feelin' bad too. Eat ye bread."

Another week passed—a difficult week of raging fevers and headaches. The last two days neither of us went up on deck. Thirty-nine day-lines had been scratched on the wall and still the ocean was endless. The excitement on this day was the sighting of a sea bird—announced to all by the sailors. "Land!"

Molly was right. We were not going to Australia.

"Move on. Move on!" The Old Man ushered us two days later. He pushed and shoved to get us from below to the deck early in the morning. "You are goin' ashore!" he announced. The girls moved quickly, excitedly, and I was caught up in the rush to the ladder. Molly, always slower, fell behind. I could not find her or wait for her.

In the chaos and utter confusion. I was told, "You're in Nova Scotia, climb in the wagon." It still haunts me. Molly was gone. Gone! Looking back at the ship and not seeing Molly was anguish, total anguish, that chipped at my soul and turned me into an obedient machine, I climbed onto the wagon.

I recall....

CHAPTER 6

I had never heard of Nova Scotia. I wanted to walk on land but after ten steps, I was pushed up into the open wagon. There were seven girls in the wagon—no Molly. We moved away from the sea, away from the small coastal village and away from the only friend I had. Maybe she's on the next wagon, I thought. But no wagon followed us.

Undefined tears dripped off my chin. There was so much to cry about that I did not care to single out a reason. They dripped unblotted and unchecked.

I tried to read the signposts along the way, sounding them out. One that I saw more than once challenged me. "Cha-Cha-an-a-d-d-da, Chanda," I concluded.

The driver, sitting to my back, overheard. "Canada," he corrected. "You're in Canada."

At a dirty mining town, we were taken off the wagon. Everything was drab unlike the beautiful country by the sea that we had come through. The houses were unpainted wood, the road was dried mud, the people mostly men, were drab, too. The only color was a small, white-washed church. Two women at a small dirty hotel ushered us in.

"Come, come girls. This way," No pushing or shoving. No animosity. As if I had been long awaited. But apprehension kept us quiet. No talking; just obedience.

The bath and hair wash renewed me, so much luxury that for a moment I forgot my fear. The feeling was compelling—body over mind. I wanted to stay in the tub, hold on to the soap, wash inside my mouth, ears, and nose. Forget who I was, where I was, why I was trembling. I got a new cotton dress. Mine was too big but each got a tie to secure around the waist.

In a small hall-sized room I ate lamb stew with potatoes and bread. Heavenly but too rich for my long-deprived body. I could only eat a small portion. I did not want to leave bread on the plate, but I did not have a pocket in my new dress.

Finally, the lady in charge spoke. "You left Ireland as girls. Now you are in Canada, and you are women. Very soon, you will have a husband to house and feed you for the rest of your life. It is your destiny." While I was trying to understand her and ponder the word destiny, she went on. "Forget the life and family you have left. You are a wife. You have a husband."

How am I a wife? Where will I get a husband?

I was so confused, I forgot to be frightened.

The door open to the outside. Men began filling the room, rushing toward the twelve little girls from Ireland. Pushing, touching, even lifting me. Turning me around. It was a terror greater than I had ever had. Men were touching my breast and reaching between my legs. It was beyond screaming or crying, I had to defend myself and fight back against the assault. Laughing and loud talking filled the air with an overwhelming feeling of attack. I began pushing hands away but there were too many. Finally, a huge man pushed others away, stepped behind me, and threw his arms across my chest, bringing my back to his belly. The giant's hands went between my thighs. I felt his erection against my buttocks. I fought to get free as an overwhelming feeling of helplessness washed through me.

"Got mine!" he proclaimed.

In reaction, I pushed back, kicked, and broke his grip. The chair behind tripped him as I fell forward. We both sprawled on the floor. The big bloat pulled himself up, shrugged, and went on to the next girl. Another man offered his hand. I stood without help and continued to back up.

"I'm Walter. What's your name?" The driver of the wagon asked.

I got to my feet, ready to defend, and unwilling to give my name.

He was a tall man, not the heavy giant I had just escaped. I was spent but ready to fight again. When he reached for my arm, I recoiled, so he pointed to a chair in a quieter place in the room. Twice he repelled anxious men asking if I was taken.

"Sit," he invited. I did, waiting for my heart and breathing to settle.

"You didn't know you were in Canada?" he asked but did not wait for a reply. "I guess you didn't know you were here to marry a miner either. I'm here to get a wife but I didn't know they were bringing children. How old are you?" My silence told him I could not talk. He paused to scratch his head in bewilderment or to gather his thoughts.

"You will have to leave this room with a man today."

I used all my power to hold back my tears as I looked across the room and saw girls being manhandled and crying.

"Might as well be me." He tried to take my hand, but I could not allow it, so he took my arm again and led me out of the room into the sunlight. I took my first walk on solid ground in forty-two days. We crossed the street and went up the hill to the little white Presbyterian church.

The clergy asked his name. "Walter Collins"

He asked my name. "Fiona Doyle."

Seven marriages were performed that day. One of them was me, Fiona Doyle, of Portumna workhouse, age thirteen years and three months, to Walter Collins, a miner from Cornwall, England.

He took me home.

CHAPTER 7

I spoke my first words to Walter Collins after we entered the house. "I am not a wife." In clear, well-formed good grammar I repeated. "I am not a wife." I had crossed the ocean and withstood an unimaginable selection process, stood before a clergy without responding to his question of intent, listened to him pronounced me a wife, and walked with this stranger into this house. "I am not a wife," I said again.

Walter made tea and brought it to the table. He poured my cup, added milk, a drop of honey and smiled as he handed it to me. I looked at his face for the first time as he sat across the table. It was a gentle face with questioning eyes, and soft smile. His tall body was very thin, and his fingernails were stained black. He had a dark short beard and receding hair. I noticed his clothes were tattered but clean. Walter Collins appeared to be old, maybe as old as Da.

I raised my head and allowed our eyes to meet. I knew I had to be somewhere. Right now, this day, I had to sit in this two-room house with a stranger and find a place for my mind and body. I pulled my legs tight together as a sign of protection. I tucked my dress tightly under my knees as if that bit of fabric could shield my womanhood. At any moment, Walter Collins could make me a wife and I knew what that meant. Terror engulfed me as I looked in the next room at the bed that held my dread. This room was for cooking, eating, and sitting by the fire. The other room would be the death of Fiona Doyle, child, daughter, sister, virgin.

He saw me looking around. "This is a two-room house. Kitchen. Bedroom. I have a well, a pump, as well as a loo out back. Wood for the fire is stacked by the door." It was a lot of talk for this quiet man who had had no one to talk to in this house for five years.

"Say something," he quietly pleaded, at a loss to make conversation.

I saw his smile and choked on the expectation in it. "No!" I screamed and stood so quickly my chair crashed to the floor. Walter caught my arm at the door. My only defense was to crumble and roll into a ball—so small that I hoped to disappear. Now, Lord, my mind pleaded. Take me, now. Walter bent down and I scooted under the table like an animal. As he reached for me, I backed into a corner. Two walls gave me comfort as I turned my head into them. "Holy Father," I lamented. I pressed so hard into the corner wall that my nose flattened, and my breath came back to me in torrents.

All went quiet and the silence calmed me. There were no sounds that Walter Collins was moving, coming, or going. The only sound was my breathing. After a minute or two, my nose came out of the corner. I needed to feel the walls, so I lifted my hands and arms to them in prayer. Silence continued and I paid attention to it. Had he left the room?

"Ma. Ma. Ma." I cried for her in hushed tones. "Patrick," my torn spirit begged. "Your Fiona…" My words were the only sounds in the room. "Help me." Sobs racked my body until exhaustion ended it all. My head, hands and arms followed the wall to the floor. When I turned to look back into this world, Walter Collins was sitting on the floor waiting.

"Fiona, we are married. I regret that you had no say in it. I could not let you run away. You have no place to go. Out that door, would you go right or left? Those walls, in that corner, give you a place. I will make your bed in that corner where you have prayed to God and your family."

Walter paused. Fiona had to understand. "Your home is here 'til you are ready to be a wife or leave it. A choice. I promise sometime in the future, you will have a choice."

He moved away and righted the chair. "Come, drink your tea. I'm sorry it is not hot, but we cannot waste it. The next cup will be to your liking." Walter sat and waited.

My shaking hands lifted the cup to my trembling lips.

"I came here five years ago to work in the mines after tin mining in Cornwall. Hoping it would be better. Not so. I go in the mines six days, rest on Sunday. Sometimes I go down at night. Doesn't matter all black in the mine anyway. Sharing what little I have will make life better for me," his explanation.

Walter was not comfortable with conversation. He could only use his few words to be honest with me.

I needed to say something to Walter Collins, but I had no words and feared I would cry if I spoke. I stood. The urge to run came again but reality or where to go, overwhelmed. I sat back down. Walter did not move. Would he let me go, I wondered. I got up again, feeling suffocated. I sucked in some air and sat again.

"Can you tend house?" he asked. "Tend a garden? Make a pot?" he said pointing to the tea and not waiting for my answers.

"I can tend a house, a garden and make tea. I've boiled potatoes over a fire."

Walter Collins came to his feet, slapped his leg in joy, and said, "Good show!" He was ecstatic. A wide grin filled his face.

"I'll move things and make your bed over there." He pointed to the corner. "No need to run. You don't have to be a wife, but I expect a partnership. Make no mistake, Fiona Collins, your young age belies all you have been through. You are not a child and will not be treated as such."

It was easy to agree to his requirements when I knew I had nowhere to run and would have a bed of my own .

"Well, Fiona, this is a good start. I'll get the fire going to make rabbit stew, with potatoes." He emphasized potatoes. "The best way to start is with some work. Don't you agree?"

I nodded, still trying to digest Fiona Collins as my name.

CHAPTER 8

I found green hills and herds of sheep not far from the house. They contrasted the brown drab of the town and comforted me. I carried rocks back from the hills. Each day, a couple of rocks, until I had built a wall around the garden that Walter taught me to tend. He quietly let me create a piece of Ireland.

The one thing we both enjoyed was hiking to the hills. Walter carved a walking stick for me to match his own. We walked together without talking. Walter was more comfortable without words. He did not take my hand but when we approached an uneven patch in the path, he took my elbow until the road was even and without obstacles. We walked on well-worn paths and sometimes forged unmarked trails. Unspoken choices, agreeable to both, were made as we hiked—where to turn, what to avoid, when to turn back.

It is hard to say when or how our relationship changed. I began to look forward to his return from the mine. I began to understand and worry about the dangers he faced in those dark tunnels. Our walks across the hill included holding hands and talking, although I did most of the talking. It was a joy to tell Walter of my family and of my expectation of seeing Patrick someday.

I recall the day he bought me a Bible and asked me to teach him to read. It was such an important day for Walter and me. Sitting and reading with Walter, close enough to feel and smell his being, changed everything. I began to want Walter to touch me, and I allowed my hand to touch his as he struggled to write words.

Walter was a good student. His skill grew quickly, and it gave me such joy. He wrote Walter Collins, Canada, Fiona… on and on. Each day new words which were easily remembered because of the way he had struggled with words throughout his life. Now he knew letters, sounds and construction and did not need to memorize words as pictures. I was overwhelmed and marveled at his mastery and quickness. One day he wrote happiness on his slate and smiled at me.

Happiness! I looked at the word with tears of joy. Happiness! When was I happy? I tried to recall early days at our cottage near Galway before the potatoes died but I could not. I could not find happiness in my whole life. Now, Walter had written happiness on his slate—happiness! For the first time in my life, I lost my breath—not for fright or anguish—but for happiness. I looked at Walter with tears in my eyes and wrote happiness on his slate.

On my fifteenth birthday, Walter Collins proposed to me.

"Fiona, will you marry me? I will go with you to the Catholic Church so we can be married by a Priest."

"Yes, Walter. I will be your wife."

EPILOG

Each morning, I get the Bible that Walter and I read, and I think of my friend, Molly. I think of the sunshine in her smile and her generous spirit that made my passage to a new life bearable. In my reverie, I must relive my sorrow when she disappeared on the dock that day. Too many partings had become a permanent, ever sad part of my life.

* * *

I had been married to Walter Collins almost eight years when Patrick came from Ireland to find me and meet my husband and three children. I knew he would come and bring news of my lost family. Patrick did not have to rescue me. He did not find Fiona Doyle. He found Fiona Collins in a happy life as Walter Collin's wife.

On new mornings, I open my Bible to read and pray for our three children, Annie, Mavis and Andrew who have grown-up and left this drab mining town.

"Please God, help my children wherever they are. Help them to find a friend like Molly Sullivan. Better yet, God, help them to be a friend like Molly Sullivan. Amen."

* * *

The undertaker is here. Walter will leave me as everyone else has. I am alone with only my memories for company. I think of Walter, my lost family back in Ireland, Molly. But

I have no need to weep. I have been trained for this role my whole life. I take comfort knowing no one—absolutely none of them—wanted to leave me.

Maybe I will cry a little before my next cup of tea.

The End

READER: If you want to know about Patrick's journey to Canada to find Fiona and the story of their reunion, it is told in *The Hungry Piper* (2019).

If you want to know about Ma's (Annie Doyle) quest to find her daughter, it is told in the pages of *The Irish Woman* (2021).

The world of thorough-bred racing pigeons is a novelty not familiar to most people. My father and his brother, Russell and Glenn Beall, were successful breeders and racers in lofts started by their father on Eleventh Street, Laurel, Maryland in 1922. Faye Beall Green presents her recollections.

This is a non-fiction and fiction piece. The story of growing up as the daughter of Russell Beall and his birds is true. Unfortunately, Russell and Evelyn died in 2001 and 1999; they were not interviewed for this piece. The author feels very confident that the words in the interviews truly represent their feelings regarding their years with The Birds in the back yard.

The Birds

By all standards, we were a normal, usual, average Laurel family—well known and respected in the community. But we had *the birds*. On the back edge of our yard, a large flock of birds lived in a well-designed coop with an aviary.

We moved through home life and school not realizing our life was different from other families in Laurel—even different from the many families we were related to—because we had *the birds*.

From the kitchen window or the deck of our home on Brooklyn Bridge Road, we could watch them fly. There were two flocks—one belonging to Russell Beall—one belonging to Glenn Beall, next door. The Beall brothers' flocks circled the houses each evening and returned to their home loft with a flutter and a few feathers—each bird to the correct loft.

We always referred to them as *the birds*. Dad had to feed *the birds*. *The birds* are out. There is a hawk threatening *the birds*. When school friends visited and wanted to go to the loft to see *the birds* we did not understand why such interest. Birds in crates in the trunk of our car were ordinary. Cooing and fluttering sounds were usual. We knew at some place along our route, the birds would be freed to fly home. The family outing was also a training mission. Very seldom did we talk of them and call them pigeons but that's what they were—pigeons. These were not ordinary barnyard or city pigeons. These were not your common pigeons degrading statues, or the nuisance birds of parks and streets. They were thoroughbred, pedigreed racing pigeons—homing pigeons—bred and trained to return to their loft at high speeds. Highly developed racers, comparable to pedigreed thoroughbred horses, going for the triple crown. Well cared for. Expensive and valuable.

The pigeons, their care and sport, were part of my life from the day I was born—even as they were to my father's youth when his father started the family sport in 1922. The lofts of my childhood are still racing today under the care of Glenn's son, Gary, my cousin. The same breed—blood lines—still racing as the Beall Loft that our grandfather started 100 years ago. A century in the sport.

In the early 50's, the birds from the Beall lofts were gaining recognition in the world of pedigreed thoroughbred racing pigeons. The sport was, and still is, global. Thoroughbred racing pigeons are a sport in the United Kingdom, Asia, Europe, Japan, Scandinavia, Africa, Australia, the Mediterranean, and South America. The Beall lofts were highly successful and well known and envied around the world.

We did not realize that our life was different because the Beall brothers were breeding and racing pedigreed pigeons. Living in brick homes, side by side, with twin lofts just yards apart on the back acre, was a great life for six cousins and un-counted pigeons, each knowing which was their home. These pigeons were trained to be either flying or in the loft. A racer that did not go immediately in the loft was a useless racer. We never had pigeons perched on our roofs, never had pigeons spoiling our windshields, never had pigeons begging at our family cookouts. Believe it or not.

The birds, like all livestock, had to be tended to daily, and our dinner was often late waiting for Dad to finish his hus-bandry tasks. No one ate until Dad came to the table. Often, he came in the house with feathers in his hair and his shoes soiled. Our mother did not like that. We had to wait a bit lon-ger while feathers, and worse, were purged. We thought we would starve.

Some Saturdays and Sundays we could not play in the back yard or have an afternoon barbeque. You guessed it…because the birds were due in from a race.

Friday events were managed without Dad because he had to crate and ship the birds. Sundays we went to church without Dad because the birds were coming in. It was life with racing pigeons. Seemed normal to us.

Doesn't everyone's father have feathers in their hair at din-ner time?

Of course not!

A bird race started on Thursday. Russell left the dinner table and went to the loft to select the birds for the race. Selection was carefully done. Entry fees are high and sending the right birds for this week's distance and conditions was important. Of the birds selected, one or more can be nominated to win. It cost to enter birds. It costs to nominate—that is betting money. Dad was in the loft a long time on Thursday—handling and inspecting each entry.

Friday was shipping night. After dinner the birds were

crated and, along with the *pigeon clock*, taken to the club in Baltimore or Washington depending on the race being entered. Bets (nominations) were placed.

The pigeon clock was inspected. The time had to be accurate. Inside the pigeon clock, the paper stamping mechanism had to produce the all-important proof of dispatch and arrival. It was inspected and sealed. Any tampering with the seal and the loft would be disqualified. The pigeons would sleep all night while the truck driver and one club member went to the designated release-point. Distances varied. All from the south, southwest or west with the prevailing winds. The longest race was about 500 miles.

Saturday was race day. Dad would get a call telling the exact release time. He would calculate when to expect his birds. Shorter races brought the birds home that day. Longer races often meant the birds would come in early on Sunday (pigeons do not fly at night). Hours before the birds were expected, our yards were closed for play. No balls, no swing set, no tag games. Dad put his lawn chair under a shade tree, got his shot gun, put a couple of 12-gauge shells on the grass. He waited, in case a hawk who regularly threatened the flock, came to the area. Next door, under another shade tree, Glenn got his chair. No need for another shot gun; Russell was the marksman today. The only sounds in the yard was the brothers' talk back and forth or the loud shout –"there's a bird"– at a distance, flying over the trees. It was impossible to know whose bird it was, but the pigeon knew. He/she flew right for its home loft. Make no mistake, Russell and Glenn were competitors. There was always pride getting the first bird and beating your brother.

When the incoming racer landed on the loft, he was trained to go in, where on race day, a trap held him. Russell ran quickly to the loft to activate the clock by removing the rubber race band, putting it in a capsule, dropping it into the slot on the clock, and turning the handle to register the time. Timing was everything. Don't run to the loft too soon and frighten the bird before he goes in. Don't fumble removing the band. No clumsy fingers filling the capsule or getting it in the slot. Races are won or lost by seconds.

The truth is the racers from the Beall loft were so successful that often the brother who got the first bird in today's race, beat all the entries from the club. Russell and Glenn took turns in the winner's circle.

It was not unusual to see a long black limousine parked on our back driveway. Men would not get out until invited by Russell. His wife, Evelyn, or the children, would alert him that a Japanese Embassy car awaited his invitation to visit the loft. Very polite and formal men in dark suits went into the feathers and droppings at the loft on the back of the property. These gentlemen were not here just to see the birds; they wanted to buy them and ship them to Japan for breeding and racing. The Japanese Embassy car came often. These men knew the Beall loft's racers and the breeding stock that was gaining recognition. No doubt progeny of the birds that flew over the Beall yards are successfully racing today in Japanese concourses.

An interview with Russell Beall

"I want to make it clear. My name is not Russell Bee-all. It's Russell Bell, if you say it correctly. I'm Scottish by ancestry and they say *bell* not *bee-all* when they see B e a l l. By the way, it is most commonly pronounced correctly in Maryland. Not so in a state where it isn't known. Excuse me, I digress. We are not here to talk about my name. We're here to talk about my pigeons.

Most people do not know anything about thoroughbred pedigreed racing pigeons. The birds in my loft are no closer to the pigeons flying free than thoroughbred racehorses are the same as wild ponies, plow horses, fox hunting mounts or fancy dressage steeds. You must understand that before I show you the birds and explain the sport.

Don't confuse pigeon racing with pigeon fancying. We breed birds for endurance and speed. Not beauty or special flight or tumbling. Speed! We want to win the race. These birds race many distances but I'm most proud of our long-distance flyers and their record. There is a lot of money to win and there are very high breeding fees to be gained by a champion. Just as horses who proved themselves, pigeons who win races, are very valuable. A good bird goes for thousands of dollars. Sometimes for many thousands. The Beall lofts have proven race winners. However, I am not breeding birds to sell.

The sport is international. Most countries around the world breed and race pigeons. I am proud to say that the birds my brother, Glenn, and I have developed, along with our friend Lou Opal, are coveted the world over. The Opal/Beall birds are winners. We get requests from all over the world to buy our birds. Also, we get requests from members of local clubs to buy birds, but we do not entertain them. Why would we do that and compete against our own blood line. Understand?

Come into the loft. Stand still. The birds will not land on you or worse. They are used to people.

This bird is a champion. He is a long-distance racer—over 500 miles. Set a record coming from Indianapolis three weeks ago. His mother was a champion, too. I have her pedigree going back longer than you can imagine. This loft and the loft of my brother, next door, was established in 1922 by our father. Our pedigree records are complete. We have been breeding and racing continually together since then.

You want to know how the races are accomplished. I know. It is the question everyone asks. We belong to two racing clubs,

Baltimore and Washington. On shipping day, usually Friday, we crate the birds we want to race and take them to the club. I might enter 8 to 10 birds. Sometimes only a few birds. Every bird requires an entry fee. I have to calculate the purse against the fees when I decide how many birds to take. The club has a truck for the crates. Drivers take the birds to the release point. Oh, I forgot…each loft is surveyed for established distance from a GPS point—down to yards. Look here is the race clock. We call it a pigeon clock. The distance calculation is registered in the clock. The timepiece is certified and sealed when we drop off our birds. The club accepts nominations (bets) on your bird. The money is recorded, and the bets are set. Each bird receives a rubber leg band—grey to be in the race, blue if nominated to win. Each band costs—blue more than grey. The club knows the exact time the birds are released. It is great having a bird win a race, even better if it is your nominated bird.

The birds are trained to go right to the loft. When they enter, tired, thirsty, and hungry, they go into a special race day trap. I run quickly to complete the certification. The rubber leg band is removed and put in a capsule to be inserted in the clock. Turn the handle to stamp the time and take a deep breath. It is exciting. You can see how important it is for a returning bird to quickly enter the loft and trap. I don't want hawks, children or weather to delay my racer going in the loft/trap. I whistle a distinctive sound to assure my bird that he or she is home. It brings him or her right in.

Sunday night my brother and I take our clocks to the club to see if we have a winner. Race weekend is over."

Interview with Evelyn Beall, wife

"Russell had the birds when I married him, and we lived on Tenth Street in Laurel. They were a novelty, and I gave them little thought. Through the years, the birds seemed to dominate our lives. I understand his hobby required a lot of time and the children and I had to accept it. Especially in the summer during race time. Our weekends had to be planned accordingly. If the children and I attended a family function without Russell, it was understood by our host—pigeon race day. I think the children did better with the birds than I did. I never went down to the loft. I paid little attention to champions, or the engraved trophies. Russell hinted at his winnings but never told us. He supported his hobby with the winnings and often surprised us with family outings and extra generosities, but I did not see the money. Racing pigeons is a very expensive sport. I'm glad it was never—never— a burden on our budget. I believe he was very successful. We have lots of trophies in the closet and a lot of distinguished visitors came to the loft. The best part was going with him to ship the birds and have dinner in a nice Baltimore restaurant. Often when he was training the birds in Howard and Montgomery Counties, we would load the kids and make a fun day in the country—picnics and ice cream cones. Sometimes, Russell brought a bag of hot steamed crabs home from his Baltimore bird meetings. I must admit those crabs took care of a lot of angst about the birds. The huge ledgers (green pages usually meant for financial spreadsheets) that Russell used for pedigree records, were on the dining room table. He spent hours recording bloodlines. They had to be moved if we wanted to eat at that table. I wonder how many times I said, 'Russell, move those books.' Or 'Russell, there's a feather in your hair!' I wonder?"

* * *

Comment from Faye Beall

I would love to walk down that hill today and enter the

loft to find my father amid his birds. I would walk in quietly, knowing the birds would accept me. He would be standing six foot tall, with a feather in his hair. I can see him….

Dad reaches over and picks up a bird. He gently holds the body in his large left hand letting the legs fall between his 3rd and 4th finger. With his right hand he strokes the head and very large chest before he lifts and spreads the wing. The beautiful light grey and blue checked hen rests in these hands as she proudly looks at her wing, too.

The End

Beall Special Eggnog

From Mr. Lou Opal (Pigeon breeder extraordinaire)

½ bottle brandy
½ bottle rum
1 lb 10X sugar
1 doz eggs
½ gal whole milk

Separate the eggs. Beat the whites and set aside. (Use a mixer to get stiff peaks.)

In another bowl, beat the yolks and slowly beat in the sugar. Continue beating pouring the brandy and rum in slowly. The alcohol will "cook" the eggs.

Fold in the egg whites and refrigerate the mix.

When serving, mix equal parts with milk and sprinkle with nutmeg.

Note: can be made glass by glass or in a large punch bowl—always equal parts with milk

Father Pleasing Dessert

Strawberry Sorbet

1 lb frozen sliced strawberries (2 ½ cups)
½ cup coconut cream
¼ cup honey
Zest of one lime

Combine in a blender at high speed. 3-5 minutes until pureed. Freeze until ready to eat. Serve a scoop over a generous bowl of Snow Ice Cream (or Breyers vanilla ice cream).

Snow Ice Cream

1 ¼ cup sugar
1 egg
1 TBS flour
Mix together to make a paste in saucepan.

Add:
1 cup whole milk
Stir to mix well and cook until thickened.
Remove from heat.

Add:
1 tsp vanilla
Blend well and allow to cool completely in freezer for about an hour. (Do not freeze.)
Stir in 2 – 3 quarts of clean SNOW!

Chasing the Evil Dog

Chapter 1

Loneliness is an evil dog. It bites at your heels urging you to do *something* at the same time begging you to curl up on a pity rug beside cold embers.

After spending all my adult life married, I do not really know how to be alone and am only now realizing how insidious and evil it is. Loneliness fills the empty space in my bed since my husband died. It stands in the middle of the living room, echoes from the corners of the hallway, and follows me into the shower where there is nothing to distract. Things are always just as I left them, and I am the only one who can put wrinkles in the air. Worst of all, loneliness constantly evaluates my life and feeds on my memories. I keep this part of my life to myself as an addict keeps his secret and his source so no one can steal the terrible commodity. I need grief, loneliness, and hunger; in return, my life is demanded in the feed dish.

My life is in fragments—light and dark. In the light, friends work to help, ironically making the dark even blacker. It is not an even division. The dark is stronger and slowly pulling me away from the light to a place where all I have is myself and my work. I am a writer.

The evil dog rises from the corner to hound me again tonight. I will not call a friend; I will not go to the club and be with people; I will not have a long visit with my sister on the phone. What is the point? Sooner or later, the empty house and vacant phone are all that is left of the day.

The bedroom is black except for the red light from the LCD glaring 1:19—telling me of two hours of sleep—the night must go on. I need sleep, the only refuge left to me. I pray for relief. Before I turn over to pull the pillow to the cool side, I realize the house is totally dark. Do I have to rouse from this half-sleep to think about the missing night light in the bathroom, the lack of reflection from the porch light? The bedroom door, usually outlined with a glow from the other parts of the house, is lost. I should check, but the cool pillow invites my head. Are my eyes closed or is the LCD on the clock out? I decide not to come awake and think about these things. The quiet and the dark are part of my refuge and I hide in it. The puzzle of time and enigmatic house is put away until the sound of the front door opening alarms me. I am sitting up when it closes.

Awake—frozen with fear. Nothing will move my legs or arms. My throat is constricted and a pain shoots from my chest, across my jaws, to my ears. Sweat wets my brow. The mechanics of breathing and screaming are lost. I hear my heart beating but I am mistaken. It is rhythmic footsteps—footsteps across the foyer. How crazy is it to take a split second to chastise myself for not investigating the dark house? A minute? An hour ago?

My brain tries to assess as my body sits in the dark, knowing my carefully planned night illuminations are gone, and fear of a house invasion is here. Now! I am in danger. I am not alone. The evil dog is driven away by some terror in the night that may or may not be worse than being alone. I am sure that whoever is walking uninvited into my house cannot be the answer to my earlier prayer.

I instinctively pull the quilt up to my throat and listen to exactly twelve footsteps as they cross the great room, ten steps faintly fall on the hard kitchen floor and seven silent ones cross the thick Persian rug in the dining room. My ears ache to hear, and my brain struggles to decide—am I awake?

A familiar sound alerts me—the latch on the liquor cabinet. It is opened, and a drink is poured. This is ridiculous. I slip from the bed to the floor and creep to the alcove by the door as is my plan if a thief or worse should enter my home. If the intruder enters the bedroom and approaches my bed, I will quickly scoot out from my hiding place next to the door and make my escape. I sit and wait, but there are no footsteps coming toward me. The only sound is the small *thunk* of a glass coming down to rest on the oak wood table. I slip under a small table in the corner where a cloth to the floor hides me. I heighten my alarm, review my escape plan, and wait for the intruder.

A new sensation comes as I cower in the dark—my death wish. Ever since my husband took his last breath and his soul departed his body, I have wanted death and release. If escape is to come this night, it will be a deal well made. My spirits take a strange twist and I begin to regret leaving the warmth of my bed where I would rather be if the stranger, drinking my husband's whiskey, could take away blackness and give me my desire. With the comforting thought of *death*, I drift into sleep, soothed as if I were being held in loving arms. I want to be turned inside out—let my cold skin be covered by hot red blood, forced by a heart—broken beyond repair.

★ ★ ★

The morning light streaming through the window makes a green and gold glow under my tablecloth tent. It was only a nightmare, and I feel a funny disappointment. The clock is lighting the time and the nightlights are waiting to be turned off for the day, as is the porch light. There is no hangover from the nightmare, no uncharted undefined emotions that might be expected. There is only a stiff neck from sleeping curled up under the table. Strange, but acceptable.

Life is good and a bit less lonely as I shower and dress to meet my friends at the SunLight Bagel Shoppe. My hair and make-up look fine, the new jeans fit great, and my friends will never know that the smile was applied as surely as the makeup and jeans. Hopefully, today's activity will fill more of the empty spaces—more than every day in the last sixteen months. A glance into the dining room unsettles me and takes away the hopeful spirit I am trying to claim. The liquor cabinet is slightly ajar and a spill on the carpet is undeniable. I let a smile cross my face as I grab a moment of denial. The liquid is blotted, and the cabinet door closed with a snap. I was in the cabinet Tuesday. Did I spill water as I tended the ivy plant draping over the cabinet? Of course, a good detective would have smelled the cloth that blotted the spill—a detective that wanted the truth. Not me. Instead, I go to the computer and review the last pages I wrote.

It is time to go for that bagel. The soaring spirit of the day feels so comfortable and so much more real than a nightmare. I laugh out loud, as I climb into the car, ignore the unsettling questions of last night, and go for the illuminated side of my life.

Chapter 2

The front door opens and brings me out of my slumber again. Last night's panic tightens my chest. I know where the footsteps will go. The clock reads 1:19, then flicks to dark. Excitement laces my fear.

My death wish comes instantly and lustily. No need to fear this grim reaper. I *want* escape from this dark life that oppresses and strangles all hope of something better. My spirits lift at the possibility, and I decide to wait in the warmth of my bed for the stranger drinking my whiskey. The cabinet opens. Liquid gurgles into a glass.

Suddenly my confidence weakens in the reality that rendering life may not be easy. How queer to worry about the manner in which he would kill. Stab me? Strangle me? Quick? I desire a milder death. How weird the thought.

Tonight's possibilities do not equate to my prayer to go to sleep and not wake. Although I want to leave this voided life, I cannot imagine the moment before death without opiates, without drugs, without sleep. The stranger in my dark house could be a welcomed voyager of death, but violence was never mine; it always belongs to someone else. Abruptly new emotions grip me. My chest tightens and pain courses through my body as it did last night. I am a foolish poet who cannot decide between the maudlin and the real. I begin to crumble. My resolve is making crumbs in my bed.

A sound breaks my reverie… a glass hits the floor. No mistake. A glass that falls to the floor without breaking makes a distinctive sound.

* * *

My eyes open to the filtered light of the rising sun. The quilt is still pulled to my throat. I clutch my heart, which is rolling in my heavy chest, and race into the dining room. My second breath is taken beside the liquor cabinet, which is secure and seemingly unbreeched. God! Why these dreams? Do I really want to be dead at the hands of an intruder? Am I so desperate? A slow float to the floor allows me to regain my composure. Sitting like a little girl at a Girl Scout campfire, I look around the beautifully appointed room, with the sunlight pouring into the southern exposure. A sunbeam lights something under the cabinet—a shot glass, still wet. I curl into the fetal position, reach my arm under the cabinet, and lay my hand on the glass, unable to rise to the day. Finally, I go to my computer and write several chapters—something I have not done for weeks.

The evil dog of loneliness has been forced to the corner. Loneliness cannot exist with excitement and anticipation brought by my night visitor.

In two days and nights, my hold on the rim of reality has slipped. The light of a seemingly good existence is yielding to the black, black night. The smell and taste of bitter liquor dripping from this glass is real and demands too much from me.

This apparition is real. He has forced me to define my life. He must have the answers to the questions storming my brain. The only thing I know is he has come to help me. Somehow.

The struggle to find footing since my husband died has affected my work. Suddenly it seems so clear. I need to write. My visitor is forcing me to use the night to write. I do not know exactly how he is connected to my writing, but he is. My book needs to be finished and published. Unrefined poetry is piling up on my desk. The new book that is walking around in my head must be committed to words. Whatever it will be, it starts today, and I cannot put it away when the sun goes down. It is impossible to understand what is happening at night in my mind and my dining room. The only sense I can claim comes with the words I am committing to paper.

I am a reasonable woman, intelligent and beyond mysticism. My dreams and sleepwalking are more than stupid manifestations. *He* is more than that.

* * *

As I sit with my manuscript fresh on the screen, my creative instincts force me to consider the wet shot glass that I found on the floor. I do not care. With amazing ease, the lines fill the pages, the pages fill the chapters, and the hours of the day pass away. The emotions of the last two nights are devoid of trepidation. Willingness to die makes a burdenless existence and brings flowing creativity.

As evening approaches, I think of bed, and my only fear is that he will not come.

Chapter 3

The porch light is on, and a beautiful fall wreath hangs in the light. Along the walk, chrysanthemums bloom in ambers and gold. Nightlights are on in the kitchen and bathroom. My clock is beaming a red digital 11:19. I am tired after a day and evening of creating chapters in my new book. Things are so normal that feelings of loneliness are at bay, almost as if the dog has become friendlier. I sleep.

I am not sure why I am sitting up in bed without a sound or motion disturbing me. Awake, not only because I want to be, but because I need to. It is not dark. The dim nightlights are breaking up the darkness into quadrants just as they were designed. The bright red digits on the clock read 1:19.

I know why I am awake.

Stepping into my slippers and robe, I walk to the doorway and look across to the dining room where he is seated at the table. Common sense tells me to be frightened and call 911, but an uncanny calmness holds me in time and space. My hands shake as I struggle with the robe zipper to hedge against the cool house.

"Is there heat?" he asks. "I feel a chill."

I see an empty glass clasped in his left hand and his head held up by the other. My bottle of Canadian Club is capped. His dark clothes speak of another century, and his unkempt hair spills through his fingers. I reset the thermostat a couple of degrees and take a seat opposite him. I study his high forehead, deep eyes, and heavy dark eyebrows. He strangely reminds me of my great uncle, but of course he is not. He is not friendly; nor is he unfriendly. I sit, waiting.

"I am here because you wanted me to come. Over and over, you have asked for my help. Well, I am here now. It is good you are not frightened; we have so much to accomplish." He filled the glass, drained the last drop, and held it like a beacon. "Remember this. Only one drink, maybe two. In case I forget and ask for more than my allotment." All is reasonable as he speaks and charges me with this responsibility.

I know who he is! How often I have talked to him about my writing. How often I have complained to him about my blocks and some of the trash I have committed to paper. How often I have reviewed his life and works. How often I have claimed a relationship with him because my mother's maiden name is Poe.

He allows time for my thoughts and continues, "You call yourself a writer. I have been reading your work and you may be a writer—just may be a great one. Without modesty, I concede, you remind me of myself except you have started late in life. Why have you been wasting your time? The point is we must hurry. Get right to work. I am not sure how much time we have."

Somehow, I know he is talking of my time, not his. He takes off his coat as the room warms. "You are meant to write at night. Even if the sun is up, it is lost on us. Dark days have nothing to do with the sun. If we are alike at all, I know this— we write in the dark with an eclipsed spirit that can escape the light of day. That is where you are now. Maybe last year or the years before you wrote in the light. Not now. You can only write where you are, my dear."

I get up, return the whiskey to the cabinet, and place the glass in the dishwasher. Suddenly I feel faint; heaviness presses my chest as a black shade dims my vision. I struggle to get my exhausted body back to bed. All is quiet, except for the sound of the front door opening and closing.

* * *

I do not need a doctor or psychiatrist; I am totally calm, and I am not crazy. There is a small bit of happiness today, and that is something I had not claimed for a long, long time. My day-time activities are not compromised but the only thing I look forward to is living in the dark with this man. And my writing.

The third morning starts with a clear head. The bed is made, and everything is in order as I make coffee and go to the screened porch. That big dog looks smaller and less hungry to-day. It is easy to put aside the dream that he sat at my table and talked to me. If those unsettling thoughts come, I concentrate on my coffee, the sunshine, and returning to my work. I have control and the dog is at bay.

The black soiled coat on the chair beside the sliding door takes me back. Good Lord! My hand trembles as I reach out to touch it. It smells like the night. It feels like a burden of years, and I am amazed that I have touched it, picked it up! As I hold the fabric of my nightmare, the doorbell rings. I head to the door with weak knees, contemplating this man invading my daytime, too.

I should have known better; he told me he is of the dark and will not come in the day.

"Are you ready?" Cassie asked.

"I forgot. Come in. Have some coffee. I will be ready in a minute."

She looked at the coat; she saw the coat. It is real!

"What a rag. Where did you get that?"

I quickly made a lie about it being on the patio this morning, most likely left by the mowing crew.

"I'd think even laborers could afford better than that. Pitch it in the garbage. Let's go."

Cassie is my friend, yet she does not want to know that I died with my husband, that I am a zombie, cavorting with an apparition every night, that the touch, feel, and smell of that old rag coat is ungluing me. I cannot explain the coat nor the fact that it is real to someone who is not part of my nightmare. Cassie does not need to know that I will not throw the coat on the curb to be picked up with my garbage. We go on with the trivial plan to shop today.

Chapter 4

Tonight will be different. I will stay up and wait. I need to prepare. First, his coat is hung on the back of the chair he prefers. Then, the bottle of Canadian Club whiskey is placed on the table with a small glass. After the evening news and Conan O'Brien, I sit at the table, with my laptop, and began writing. Waiting is easy until 1:00, between television and working on my book the time goes quickly. The last nineteen minutes are more difficult. All the lights are off except the porch light, the nightlight in the bathroom and the small light on the refrigerator are turned off. I am ready.

1:09. 1:10. 1:1... My head falls to the table.

"Wake up," he says. "We have work to do."

I look up and smile into deep eyes that seem to caress me, and I know he is as happy to see me as I am to see him.

"Let me remind you, I am here because you want me here. Your writing is my mission. The chapters you did yesterday are the best you have ever written. Don't look so surprised. I have read everything, even the words you wrote tonight. Believe me, it is easier to read your work than to break the plasmic plane and come here. Much easier. Let us begin here," he says with his finger on the last sentence on the screen. "I would prefer you give me your writing on paper; I don't like this light with the words on it," he complains as he points to my computer screen.

I sit shaking my head slowly from side to side. This is too much for me and I wonder if I can write while he is intriguing my mind, challenging my soul, and causing my body to scream. When I look at him, I am not sure what I want.

His hands take my head to stop its back-and-forth motion. His warm touch to my head seems to stop the universe. "Here is the problem. You want me here and I have come. You want to be with me because you know I am the helpmate you need to be the writer you are meant to be. At the same time, you want relief from your loneliness and missing your husband. Since I am your *longing*, you have to decide—exactly what am I to do here? Are we writing or comforting each other? I suggest you pour me a drink."

It is a relief to rise from the table and do as he asks. No one can replace the love I lost. I want him to help me, not soothe me. "I will help you with your writing, teach you about critics and the deadly magazine editors. Never, never write for critics, publishers, or the public! I have waited and waited for words to pour forth from another generation and at last they are coming from you. I have seen journalist and essayist from our stem, but none have struggled with the creativity I have been looking for. Now you are ready. You are ready to show how the human condition feels, thinks, hopes, and dreads. More than that, you are ready to show the dark side—the not so soft side. Put your soul on paper. You are afraid; I know that. I was afraid… terrified. There is only one cure for our terror. Passion! You can do it; you have the passion, and I am here to make sure you don't abandon it. We are family, you see."

My thoughts race at his words. *Family? Family?* This man

who can chase the dog away; this man who invades my fears is claiming me as family. I feel warmed at his compliments, thinking I am part of his family of authors, which somehow includes me. He counts me as part of an author's society and although I am not positive of his authority, I accept my rhetoric place within this embrace of *family*.

"We are of the same family, literally not figuratively! "He pronounces angrily. His eyes flash, and his voice lowers to a special disquieting emphasis. "I am not speaking of a rhetorical family!"

He is angry at my thoughts! He is answering my unspoken words, reading my mind. I will run in alarm from this nightmare to my refuge. I cannot do this. I am losing touch with reality....

Again, he answers my thoughts. "Stay. Nothing matters but your work. Not you, not me. You must write or you will lose everything. You have suffered enough to do it. Now is the time—tonight. You are at that low point where there is only one way to go. I know the way. Stay. Do not run."

I sit at the computer and work through dawn and into the day. It is almost noon when I stumble to bed, exhausted and spent. Hunger wakens me at 4:30 in the afternoon—hunger and the nagging phrase: *We are family*. I sink back and draw the quilt over my head so I can remember the words without being a part of the light in my bedroom. ...*not a rhetorical family*. I see his face, animated and angry. A trip to the bookcase will affirm what I have come to know—what I have really known for days. Among the many volumes of classics are six collections, biographies, and old publications of Edgar Allan Poe, many of them with the famous portrait of unkempt hair and deep brooding eyes. I am looking with complete surrender at my night visitor. As long as I can remember, the family tradition has been that we are related to the greatest American writer. My grandfather's name was Poe. My grandmother's maiden name was also Poe. Our family reunions each year are full of Edgars and Edgar Allans of all ages, in each generation. He and I, as well as my children, are in the family tree that is published and recorded in the Library of Congress. Suddenly I know a lot about this night caller, and of course, I know… he is dead.

The work at my computer is amazing. It warms me and satisfies me as no other effort ever has. The inspiration to continue is burning. With a pot of coffee, a peanut butter sandwich, and indigestion that moves from my stomach to my throat and sets heavy on my chest, I spend uncounted hours writing. The story in my mind is coming to the page with new energy. My words are passionate and demanding. Exhaustion tears at my body bringing the old familiar nagging chest pain. I try and try to keep my eyes open, but the struggle is too much and the body yields to the need to sleep completely and thoroughly, to rest from the work but more importantly, to rest from loneliness that lurks in the corners, waiting to pounce.

Chapter 5

"Poetry," he demands as I walk into the house from my weekly outing with friends for dinner. The room is dim, and I am startled to be greeted in such a way at such a time. The last thing I expect when I open the door from the garage is him sitting in the dining room.

"Poetry," he repeats, "is the true measure of an author. I believe a writer must be able to express poetically before attempting to create the human story in the pages of a novel." His greeting words are warm, his eyes soft. Tonight, he is in new clothes and his hair is gently parted and combed smooth. His collar is enclosed in a soft green cravat that enhances his hazel eyes. There is a slight smile, which goes to my inner being. His improved, handsome demeanor and smile excite me as I slip out of my coat and hurry to my seat at the table. He spreads my manuscript before us.

"Pour me a whiskey, please," he asks in a most polite way.

I delight in condescending to his wishes and recall how much I loved doing things for my husband. As the aromatic liquid fills the glass, I want to do for this man small comfort things to keep him as he appears tonight and make sure he does not go back to the haggard man of the past nights.

He senses my desire to turn on the light switch and cautions me by raising his hand in a halting gesture. The drink is downed in his usual manner.

"I am impressed at the work you have done on your novel, but I hope you realize it is in its infancy. Get your story done quickly so you can go back and develop your characters until you hate the ones that must be hated and love the ones that are personifications of yourself." He pauses to draw his fingers through his thick hair and take back to himself the words of wisdom he is proclaiming. With a twisted smile, he continues. "I will admit though, that I hated the characters that were really me, but that is a basic difference between us. A good difference, which I think will keep you from being consumed by yourself. Do you know which are which?" As usual, he does not want or expect an answer. "I was consumed by my characters. They ate me up until there was nothing left. I felt smaller and smaller...." His voice drifts off. "Poetry saved me...well, it saved me as long as it could..."

As the twilight dims, we work on the characters until he is satisfied, and I am astounded at how close I am to perfection with each one. Time is undefined, stretching out endlessly, and I do not know how long we worked. We have enough light to do whatever he wishes but the air seems old, stale, and going thin. It is hard to breathe. The only two things alive in the room are his voice and his words.

I cannot find any reason to deny my infatuation with him. I do not need light or oxygen. My work and I will feed on a strange sustenance that he is providing. A restless impatience to create causes me to wrap up my thoughts and feelings in a neat package, but he will not allow me to push or pull.

"No. No. Let it happen to your story, to your characters and to your readers. Let time and place wait. Give it breath—let it breathe. Never wrap up a story too soon and never, never wrap up a poem. That is why we covet readers. Readers do not want *the end*. They will not look forward to the last line or last page—if you are a good writer."

"Let us share a whiskey," he suggests quietly.

For the first time in my life, I drink a shot of whiskey. I feel the hot spirit go down my gullet and the harsh, pleasant liquor washing through my body instantly diluting my inhibitions.

"Put it away," he says, as he pushes the bottle and wipes his mouth with a beautiful linen handkerchief monogrammed P. "Love me. I am your talent, not your lost husband. You must embrace your talent, respect it, and believe in it. We shall be in love from this moment on. I remind you; our time is short. I am not replacing anyone. At last, you have no fear of your talent. Listen to me," he insists, but already has my undivided attention. "I will save you from your demons, from loneliness, and allow you to work in the dark. You will show me that you can work in the light, too. The poor bastard untalented writer must choose between the dark and the light; you do not have to. You can create whichever you need. When you are writing, you will welcome me, and I will never leave you. Loneliness is fear; fear is gone."

My impatience and restlessness seem to retreat as I listen. Work, time, and space are reclaimed. The room is warm. The dog is gone.

"Nothing helps the monsters to consume like lubrication of distilled gold. Whiskey is not the devil, but it invites the devil. Careful. You can beat the terrors, or you can learn to live with them, but when you decide to let them in—they become you. One can never escape from oneself. Never. I tell you because I could not. Unfortunately, I cannot teach you about living, but this you must believe—you are a writer. Your talent is a gift, and you have nothing to fear." He pushes the bottle back to me and with a shaking hand, lifts his glass over to wordlessly ask me to fill it, breaking his own rule.

I refill both glasses and we drink again. He looks me in the eye for the first time and I return his gaze. I have a feeling of excitement, of anticipation, of exhilaration as he wordlessly directs my thoughts to my work. I have rapture, and for the first time in my life, I believe; I claim; I am a writer .

I am compelled to write. Maybe it is the whiskey that has infused my whole being with a zealous desire to write, write, write.

"Wait," he shouts and bangs his fist to the table so hard the two empty glasses fall over. "You do not understand what whiskey can do. It will inoculate you with heroic powers to create. You will go to the heights and the elixir will drop you like a red-hot coal into ice water." Anger crosses his face and reddens his eyes. I cower with that undefined pain that comes with hurt feelings.

"I must tell you what not to do as well as what to do. No false creativity. Your whole being cannot be writing. It cannot be allowed to be your life because too many paragraphs formed, while searching for the right words, are trash. Shall we say fifty percent? Maybe seventy-five percent are trash. Life can become waste if that percentage is trash Do you understand what I am telling you? You must live too. I cannot help you do that; Lord knows, I failed. I cannot teach you about dying except to say neither is easy. Desire or longing has nothing to do with living or dying. They are no part of the equation. Writing is where you are when living or dying are not important. Success is not publication; success is believing in your talent and using it to pour your soul into your manuscript a word at a time."

He pauses as if moving to some dark corner of his mind—a place that excludes me. Rejection clouds my face, and I recall, in even the purest relationship, at times, someone must be left behind, abandoned, or denied. When he comes back to me, I am able to draw a breath as if it had been minutes since I had done so.

"Tonight, let's get to poetry. I have great concern that you are worried about what people will think of you if they read your poems. That stifles you."

How does he know this about me?

"You must decide who you are writing for. More importantly—what are you writing for?"

He gives me some technical advice as he goes over my lines. At times he throws my pages on the Persian rug declaring, "Where is the point? Where is death? Poetry is about death. Call it dark, black, cold, or mystic. Call it fear . . .call it a black bird, or call it silence. Call it loneliness—whatever you like, but remember you are talking about only two things in poetry. The struggle to be warm—the womb, and the struggle not to be alone—love . . .and when you are cold and alone you are dead. Read your words. Do they satisfy you? If not, burn them."

His vehemence stuns me. Never again will I be frightened by that deepest part of myself. I will write poetry. Every word I write is justified and it only matters what he thinks. Because he is here; he is mine, and I am free with him on this plane.

The next morning, I am in the glow of his words. I begin to think in alliteration and rhyme. My mind keeps a meter, my heart burns with feeling, The keys on my computer grasp my ideas. After hours of pouring my soul onto the screen, I walk away from the computer to pick up a book and read his poems again.

The whole day has gone without torment, and I am relaxed enough to fall asleep holding *The Complete Poe*.

Chapter 6

He lifts the book from my hands, and I awake to his laughter. "Excellent choice!" he proclaims. " I hope you are reading my lines and not the commentary. Such rubbish. How can this idiot evaluate my poems for you? You are yourself a Poe with lines to write. Only a poet can critique a poem, and the *better* the poet, the *better* the opinion. And you are the best poet to judge my lines. That is my opinion." He is agitated, speaking loudly and nervously pacing the room.

I go to my seat at the table, and when he joins me, he is more settled. He does not ask for a drink, but instead turns the pages of the book until he finds *Annabel Lee*.

"Here," he thrusts the book at me and begins to recite his own words. Nothing in life can prepare me for this: Edgar Allan Poe reciting *Annabel Lee*. Tears roll down my face as I feel his passion, his pain. Like a stabbing knife it slices into my chest, bringing familiar pangs to my heart. I bite down on my lip hard enough to cause a drop of blood to fall on the page. A scarlet blot covers the line that reads—*Chilling and killing my Annabel Lee*.

He cries with me. Our eyes are red. His tears are black. Everything in the room is red and black. Virginia Clemm and my own dead husband are in a mixed vision with the blood stain on the book. A curtain falls across my eyes as I sink to the floor unable to breathe. My heart breaks again.

* * *

The sun reaches me, my swollen lip, and my bloody pillow when morning comes again. The book is lying beside me, open to the poem and so I read *Annabel Lee* again. I must read it again as I have hundreds of times. I want to find him, but instead, I find myself.

The book is new to me even though it is worn from my hand turning its pages. The words are gifts to me. So, I take many hours to read and re-read his verses. They are different today. I had denied—over and over—that the evil dog was universal. His loss was as hard as mine. EA Poe has his own mongrel—as evil and insidious as mine.

By evening, four poems are completed and on my desk. I write into the night until finally weariness forces me to sleep, and I have my first full night of rest in many.

The morning is dreary, and I sleep past my usual hour, and sit up with a start. Something must be wrong. My night visitor did not come. The lights are undisturbed, the liquor cabinet is not breached . . .nothing . . .absolutely nothing is amiss in the room. The feeling is disappointment. It is so easy to slip back to where I was before he came. The dog growls and waits for me. The long rainy day stretches before me without hope. I cannot recall what elated me just hours ago. I cry for myself, for my husband and for him. I cry as I turn off the nightlights and porch light with a sadness that reminds me of my first few hours of grief months ago. A nipping at my heels alarms me as I move to the coffee pot and go to gather my poems. The brew fills the dim kitchen with aroma and just a hint of promise. Something good can be poured into the morning if I wish it. So, I kick back at the dog.

Pages from last night are neatly piled on the desk. I re-read my words and feel comfort in their completeness. They satisfy me. I can feel him at this table. Then I notice the fine penmanship in a gothic style along the margin and I let out my breath. Seeing his hand on my pages lightens my mood. The most important notation is:

These lines give me pleasure. I could read them unsigned and know they are your words.
EAP

The nightly visits are over. He will not come again. I know with absolute assurance. His dark essence will not pervade the room again. His talent will not challenge mine again.

I will write about our time together. Most will think I am writing a fantasy; few will believe that I am writing the truth—unless they read the verity in my new work.

For un-noted weeks, I work. All social requirements are set aside so I can work. Writing hardly allows me to care for myself—eating, sleeping, grooming are neglected. The compelling desire to get my thoughts on paper overwhelms. One more line, one more paragraph, one last verse. My encounter with Poe is burning in my chest, and I write of the two men in my life—confused in my mind. My memories demand space: my work demands my life. The stories are easier and easier to write. Words pour forth fast and I have the sensation of racing. I type and type until I know it is done. The ache in my wrist meets the old nagging pain coming down my left arm from the shoulder. I feel faint. I am short of breath. Still my work continues. The pain worsens in my chest. Nausea turns my stomach. Sweat pours down my brow. Clutching my chest with both arms.

My life is surrendered to my manuscript.
Both are finished.
The evil dog wanders away with the last beat of my heart.

The front door opens. He walks twelve steps across the great room, ten steps gently fall on the hard kitchen floor, and seven silent ones cross the thick Persian rug. His hand lifts my elbow. He leads me out the front door.

The End

My mother was a good and successful woman, but she had a shaky start. Here are the true reflections of a three- or four-year-old—me. The story begins when I am 60 years old.

The Cloudless Sky

The stream of sun coming into the room is a lie—its brightness is false in this place where death is expected . The hospital room is painted green. That is supposed to be soothing and restful. Maybe it is to the person dying, but not to me. Green is the color of spring, not death, and I have a soul that will not allow me to belie the sun and hate my favorite color. I begin to find hope in this place where my mother, my tireless champion, will die very soon.

Mama is very still, but looking carefully, there is a slight rise and fall of her chest. Her face is peaceful; the sheets are neat and unruffled. The pillow looks fresh and cool as it gently cradles her head of fine straight grey hair that lifts with its only wave above her right brow. She and I are in this moment, in a room that is not for living but for tending. I would feed her, brush her hair, or straighten her bed linens if that would make her happy. But she has no requirements now except to know I am here and would do those things if she wanted. She and I have everything we need.

A walk to the window reveals a cold, cloudless December sky. By gazing straight up, the parking lot is not part of my view. "Cloudless," I whisper, but the still form is unhearing and unaware. Close to the window, the dusty vertical blind is behind my peripheral vision, and I see the cloudless sky, which is perfectly blue and slightly lighter on the horizon. It is a surprise to see the horizon, visible from the fourth floor of the hospital. And I do not think I ever saw the horizon in my hometown before. Horizons are impossible to see from a small busy life, in a small busy, level, and heavily treed town. The sky lifts my spirit over the trees, over the parking lot, over the town, over my life, over the sadness, and over the constant sound of her oxygen.

"The sky is cloudless, Mama." It is silly; she cannot hear or see. I pull the curtain and step aside, so nothing is between her and the view out the window.

* * *

The blue sky takes me back to another cloudless day. She was in bed that day, too. How long had she been in the bed? She was there for my third birthday, the 4th of July and soon it would be Halloween. I heard someone say *nervous breakdown*, but I could not see anything broken on Mama. She looked unhappy but not broken.

I wished she would get out of bed, as she should—in the morning like me. Come to the dinner table like me. Get dressed. Come outside.

I recall sometimes she helped me up on the bed with her frail hand under my arm. My doll and quilt came with me. On the bed, I was at home with her, and the bonnets and ducks stitched on the quilt. "Are you going to sit still?" she asked and smiled at my positive nod. I tried to sit still and keep her smiling, but soon, our fun brought a cloud over her face. Then she lay back on the pillow and turned her back to me. I wiggled to the floor, took my doll, my quilt and went looking for something else to do. The fun was over.

Every day was wrong, and I wondered what I could do to make it right. She wanted me there, and she wanted me gone. It was easy to walk to her bed at any time. It was in the living room. Furniture rearranged.

112

I learned to peek in to see if it was a *good time*. If her hand covered her eyes, if all the covers were thrown back, and she was kicking her legs, I would back away. When soft crying drifted from the doorway, a sad feeling made me sit quietly on the floor in the hall. I wanted to be left alone just like Mama did.

The doctor came before lunch and I made myself scarce while he was in that room, not willing to risk being given some medicine, too. When he left, I checked to see if he had brought some miracle in his black bag that would bring her back to laughter and to me. He did not.

* * *

The story of her illness was never told but through the years understanding came as family secrets became knowledge. She married to get out of a home where alcohol and abuse raged. How fortunate that the man she married was a good, hard-working, loving man. However, she was too young, and two pregnancies came quickly. Now, she lived with a nervous fear that took her sleep and kept her in the bed. They called it a *nervous breakdown* and treated it with rest, hand pats and tonics. It is hard to know if having our grandmother in the household was a help or hindrance. She kept the home going and the children cared for, so Mama did not have to care for us. She could stay in bed. Why wasn't she happy? Often her blessings were counted out to her, and she was told, "You should be happy." There were many long periods of time behind the veil that held her life together and I often thought I should go into her dark places with her, but as sick as she was, she would not let me do that.

"Take Faye to play," was one of her few demands. I was ushered out.

* * *

One day I wandered into to her room. Mama's blanket was neat, her face uncovered. I wanted her to tell Grandma to skip my nap. I was looking for a champion. Hope swelled in my chest, tempered with many disappointments.

Her smile was wonderful, and I knew, at this moment, she was glad to see me—even seemed to be waiting for me.

"Pull back the curtain, Faye, so I can see the sky." I held the curtain and pushed my back into the wall so she could see past me, from the bed to the window. "Do you see a cloud?"

I looked straight up above the tree and shook my head.

"Not one?" Mama asked.

My head went from side to side.

"It is a cloudless sky," she announced and got out of bed.

* * *

How perfect is this memory? Which of the many times I went to her bed did she ask about the clouds? Did she get out of bed that moment? I truly do not know but the two are locked together in my mind. My dream came true on a cloudless day— Mama got out of bed, started her recovery, and became the wonderful, ever-present mother she was meant to be. *Cloudless* became my magical word, and throughout my life, pure skies, without clouds, have been my spirit-lifting signs.

Here it is—another cloudless day and Mama will not stay in that bed—she is going to die. Am I supposed to be cast into the depths because of that? The marvelous healing that will come to-day is as much a mystery to me as that day many years ago when I was a little girl pulling the curtain back to reveal the cloudless sky. Mama was resurrected then ... and now, will be again.

The End

From This Place

Do not tell me to go on
It is too much to ask
For all I have in this time and place
I am not ready to pass.

Do not insist that I look up
For I need to look back
Ahead right now are roads
Seemingly long and black.

You are sure of me
And offer your hand
Myself, I have no security
A fragile strand.

Go on ahead of me
Give me a chance
To pace myself from this place
And find a tune to dance.

This story was submitted and accepted for publication in the 2023 edition of the *Bay to Ocean Journal: The Year's Best Writing* from the Eastern Shore Writer's Association. "Bread Pudding" has been nominated by the *Bay to Ocean Journal* editors for a Pushcart Prize which honors the best literary writing from small presses and publishers. The Pushcart Prize is one of the most prestigious literary awards.

Bread Pudding

Our friendship was easy and strong, no demands and no issues. He was handsome, wild, and non-conforming, truant, trouble. I was popular, a class leader, rule follower, conformist. High school kids. A couple, but not within the definitions allowed in school. Not romantic, not dating, just always seen together. Safe without demands. The school staff questioned my relationship with him. We knew what the opinions were, and we ignored them. We were young and we could ignore. There were very few boundaries and no definitions to our friendship. Two young people who liked to be together. Sometimes he quickly kissed me.

Graduation was called commencement in the late '50's. It was a beginning and the speeches from the podium, on that hot, non-air-conditioned June day, proclaimed new life, new opportunities, new freedom. But he was one of the graduates sweating and not listening under his cap and gown. He did not feel *a new life or new opportunities*, only a new freedom, which he could not fathom. Freedom. The first thing he would do was render that to a drill sergeant. He was going in the Army.

"I'm going in the Army on Friday. What are you doing tomorrow? I have one day. Let's do something."

He did not want to spend his last day with the girl who was going to cry and moan about him writing to her and coming back to her. He did not want to spend the day with the easy girl who would spread her legs for him. There would be plenty of that along the way. He wanted to be with me but did not quite know why. Just an easy choice.

The plan to spend the day together came rather nonchalantly when we were entering into the city swimming pool. The day after graduation was even hotter. The all-night parties left most graduates wanting to laze around the aqua water and be together one more day before *commencing*.

Could it be that we were holding on to the one thing we learned yesterday—the knowledge that we and our classmates would never be together again after 12 years? Our class was small, fifty-seven in 1957. We were almost a clique. Within that clique, he and I were part of a core of students that had traveled together since first grade. He and I were a tight inner group and even more so because we lived on the same road and saw each other outside of school, too. He was going to miss me, and I was going to miss him. He did not realize it but this one day was to assure him that I would always be on our road, at the same phone number and walking the same streets while he was gone.

"I'll always be here," I promised.

He called me when he got out of the Army. He called me when his grandmother died. He called me when he got married. Divorced. Married. Divorced. He called when he was diagnosed with cancer and when he was cancer free. He called me when he put his life back together. He had some interest in my life and family, but not much.

Fifty-five years after graduating, he called me to tell me he was very sick. His cancer was back. "I'm not going to beat it this time."

I promised years ago that I would always be here for him. A promise of youth and naivety, but I did not expect, after so many years, that he would want me to fulfill that promise. But he just wanted to talk. Easy.

I lived a state away and could not incorporate him into my life now. I was a widow and had begun a literary career. He brought me up on his story and asked for mine. During the next weeks, he called often.

"Bread pudding," he said, his voice noticeably weaker. "Custard topped bread pudding like my grandmother used to make."

I looked up my recipe and resolved to make it for him. But he was so far away, and I delayed. We talked and again I thought, *I'll make that bread pudding*. It was so easy to go back to my busy life after hanging up the phone. Bread pudding was nagging me, but I kept putting it off.

I do not know why, on that particular Wednesday, weeks after he asked for it, I made bread pudding—custard topped—and packed a cooler. Today I would drive from Delaware, over the Chesapeake Bay—130 miles—and take his wish to the nursing home deep in Southern Maryland.

The nursing home and his room were exactly like thousands of others. Generic and almost clean. Antiseptic to blanket a smell. A cheery bulletin board and a pitcher of ice water. One window. One chair.

He was surprised to see me sitting, quietly waiting for him to wake up.

"What are you doing here?" he asked with astonishment and happiness all over his face.

"Bread pudding," I replied.

He was weak and had little appetite, but he wanted his portion. I helped him to sit up and eat. We each had a creamy, rich, nutmeg flavored, sugary sweet, bread pudding with custard on top. Just like he remembered.

"Exactly right," he said.

He did not eat much but the renewal on his face belied his fate and took me back to the handsome boy of 1957.

"Cancer is burning me up." He told me he was hot as he handed his bowl back. I got a cool cloth and wiped his head, back, chest and arms to take the fever down. It was the first time I had ever touched his body.

We talked of old times and how important we have been to each other. He said he loved me, and I knew, in some ways, I loved him, too. "I love you, too," I told him. We had what was our allotted devotion. A love that fulfills promises—eventually.

We enjoyed each other in this generic nursing home room where announcement on the speaker interrupted his sleep and the pulsing oxygen helped him to relax. He opened his eyes often to make sure I was still there.

"Are you a dream?"

"Hardly...you ate my bread pudding."

One last smile before his medication ended our day. I kissed him and said good-by.

He died on Thursday.

The End

Custard Bread Pudding

4 eggs (beat well)
¾ cup sugar
1¼ tsp. vanilla
1 lg. can Pet Evaporated Milk
2 cups whole milk
4-5 slices of bread* buttered both sides; broken into pieces
Nutmeg

Combine with a whisk – eggs, sugar, vanilla, and both milks.

Beat well for several minutes until the sugar is dissolved.

Pour in a 1-1/2 Qt. Casserole Dish

Gently mix bread to wet. It will float on top.

Sprinkle with nutmeg.

Set casserole dish in a pan of hot water in oven

Bake at 350 degrees until set – 1 hour and 6 minute

*Recipe calls for day old white bread; however, I have used whole wheat; sometimes fresh; sometimes not - it doesn't seem to matter. Use 6 slices of bread if you do not want custard on top

Lost Point

Chapter 1

Things had to happen this way. My brother Al was dead. Over the last decade I had known, unless I died first, this was exactly how it would go down. Without maneuvering around it, when the time came, I would pick myself up from this independent life, think of my strange bit of family and drive to Lost Point. Forget flying. The closest airport was Raleigh, two hundred miles from Lost Point, and taking a cat on an airplane was a hassle.

The Capitol Dome, the Washington Monument, and the beautiful city outside my window was my comfort zone and not easy to leave. I petted Lucinda and put her in the cage for the trip.

"Maybe it will go quickly," I thought, knowing things never worked out easily for me. My co-worker's answering machine at the State Department would inform the one person who would miss me.

"Ed. Sandy. My brother has passed away in North Carolina and I will be gone at least a few days. I'm leaving now. The Malta file is locked in my top drawer, and you can reach me on the cell. I'll call on Monday. Sorry. I have to go."

All those important state issues that made my life were now being easily passed off to someone else—almost like rendering a part of me. There was no one else to call. In the hall mirror, I saw an aging prom queen looking back at me as I put some graying hair behind my ear. *I hope Ed doesn't screw it up*, I thought as the door locked behind me.

The suitcase was light: a proper outfit for a funeral, shorts and tops for the already summer weather in North Carolina. With the suitcase, my pillow and Luci-the-Cat packed into my SUV, I left to face death again, seven years and eight months since the Twin Towers became Bill's tomb. Some terrorist flying a jet made me a widow, and my work became my life. This trip to Lost Point forced me to recall the trip to New York on September 11, 2001. *At least this funeral will be quick*, I mused, looking for the only positive,

The dread of being alone, losing my only family member, swamped and surprised me because I could not think of anything my brother had done to keep me from feeling alone all these years.

With my hand on the key, I took a deep breath, and started the engine. We headed south and ran into rain on the Richmond bypass. Rain seemed to suit my mood as five hours driving stretched before me into the depths of Pamlico County. Actually, the drive is easy once you get off Interstate 95 just over the Virginia/ North Carolina line and head into Martin and Beaufort Counties—no traffic; only farm equipment hogging the road. Unfortunately, we had to bypass the familiar turn on Route 64 to the Outer Banks where Bill and I spent many happy days. "I wish we were going to the Banks," I whispered to Luci. Our path continued further south but still along the coast.

The next turn was east on Route 33 into Pamlico County and all pleasantness melted from the landscape. I avoided thinking about what waited for me at the end of the road until the dark feelings came again with this turn.

The hope of spending some time with Al was always with me but I had stopped beating myself up over his reluctance to barely acknowledge me. Birthday and Christmas cards had kept alive the possibility that we could resume our childhood relationship—the time I remember as good—the only memories I could ever go to. If only some kind of a falling out or disagreement had drawn a parameter that I could understand. However, there were none—just the gradual darkening of our relationship and drifting into a fog of non-association. One thing's for sure, I was his only relative, and the things just ahead of me—the things he left behind, including his money and Lost Point, didn't mean anything to me. They just had to be dealt with.

In this sea level area, the water crept to the road on a northeast wind and the feeling of going down and down was pervasive. Over the last 45 miles, we traveled to sea level from an elevation of maybe ten feet. Expecting the ears to pop was ridiculous, it was not an incline, we were descending. We were coming down in mood. The rain continued to beat on the windshield and the water lapped the little bridges and covered the road in spots as we crossed Route 306, the last possible road to *somewhere*. It had been a long time since I had traveled this road, but nothing changes down here, "…where farmers still believe in tobacco," I remarked to the relentless rain. Luci answered me with her emerald eyes and begged with longing meows, to be let out. "It won't be too soon now." But she did not get the double-innuendo.

A blue ribbon tied to Al's mailbox flapped in the breeze, reminding me that Anita believed it brought good luck. Anita! I had not thought of her until this moment. Anita! The only person in Al's world. She kept a blue ribbon on the mailbox and replaced it regularly when it faded. She always had her long white hair tied with the same good luck charm.

The driveway into Lost Point was sandy, and the pine needle cover made it slippery in the rain. It was long and overgrown. The narrow tire tracks bounced me in the right or left groove. The uneven wobble seemed appropriate for my approach. Obviously, the golf cart was the only vehicle that had used this trail regularly from the house to the mailbox.

Pine trees reached out and made a terrible screeching noise against the bright red paint of the car. Lucinda jumped in terror at the sound. "Now, now, Luci. It's alright, baby," I purred. The cedar shingle house was almost lost in the overgrown shrubs surrounding it. The screen was off the porch and the door kept banging in the wind. I had a quick fleeting recollection of this place when I last saw it in 1985. I tilted my head over to look around the corner as if to assure myself that the Pamlico River was still flowing beautifully just beyond the house. A note on the door flapped in the wind.

"Use Your Key."

"Anita! Anita! It's me, Sandy." I announced.

No sound came back to greet me. I pushed some clutter aside, set the cat carrier down, and went back to the car to get my pillow, suitcase, and the litter box. I needed a moment to breathe deeply before reentering the house. Clutter was a kind word to describe the scene before me. Dust invaded my nostrils and the dampness of the rain made me feel like I was breathing mud. The light switch failed to add light to the cloudy illumination coming in the big window. Click, click sounded the switch.

"How stupid!" I told Luci. If it did not work, repeated switches would not bring the light.

Clutter was everywhere, with hardly a path to travel from one room to another. I wove my way around books, magazines, and newspapers in stacks. Boxes, formed canyons—each with scribbling on the sides. Piles and heaps of *things*! There was amazing organization in the horror of it. All the magazines together. Many lamps over here. A pile of men's clothes in this corner, not to be intermingled with the pile of women's clothes over there. Vases together; artificial flowers tied in bunches. I could not comprehend the organized mess.

There was no sign of Anita.

I picked my way from room to room, gently calling her name. The dining room table and chairs that came from our family home in Maryland, and the organ that had once been in our living room, as well as the picture that hung over the mantle, reminded me of my childhood. It was with dread that I headed toward the bedrooms, fearful that I would finally find Anita, but she was not in either one.

The most surprising room was the spotlessly clean kitchen. It was uncluttered and ready for meal preparation ."Dishes, glasses, mugs, Campbell's soup, pasta, and cereal," I announced as I checked the cabinets. Two placemats and napkins at each side were on the table.. I drew a glass of water and sat down to regroup, automatically hitting the light switch. Surprisedly, the light came on. It was then that I noticed the note scribbled on the small chalkboard by the door. "Shrimping." I explained to Luci, "Shrimping is done at night," amazed that I would recall that.

It was nice to see the clean kitchen and discover that the little powder room next to the garage was clean and useable. The refrigerator had milk with a current date, so I ate a bowl of Cheerios to take care of hunger pangs that mixed with the unsettled feeling in my stomach.

The problem of where to sleep nagged at me. It was time to face my first problem. Where would I lay my head and make myself comfortable for the night? The sun was going down. It would be dark in the bedrooms soon.

There were no linens on the beds. The best plan was to clear things out of one room and sleep in my clothes under the afghan I kept in the car. The room I chose was full of fishing equipment. At least 20 poles were leaning in the corner and the pictures leaning against the bed were fishing scenes and fish portraits. Over by the window, tackle boxes were stacked just as a child builds alphabet blocks. If I was careful not to bump it, the pyramid could stay there overnight. The pictures and the pile of fishing vests and hats had to go into the great room. It was a job, but finally the clutter was moved from around the bed to melt into the mess in the great room. The bed was cleared, and my nest was made for the night. My tired head lay easily down on my familiar pillow. My eyes closed as I said a prayer of thanksgiving to God that it was not hot enough to need air conditioning on this night in May. Expecting sleep to rush on me, I asked Him for strength and reminded Him that I was weak.

Down here, there is no illumination at night, no streetlights or neighbor lights. Dark is black and I was not even sure if my eyes were open.

The prayers were barely finished when thoughts that I had avoided came and filled my black room and mind. Thoughts were bouncing. *Where is Anita? Where did she go after she called me? What happened to Al? How did he die? How will I work through all this muck? How long must I stay here? What is the law in North Carolina? Were Al and Anita married? Is common law marriage recognized here? Where is the money—it cannot be ignored—and what will I do with it? Where is Anita? What were her words, exactly?*

With my head turned to the window, I saw a small light across the water. It became my lighthouse and I needed it to keep the rocks in my path from taking me down.

I struggled to focus my wide-awake mind back to yesterday when Anita had called. She was very clear speaking; better than the last time we spoke. I wonder where she called from. No phones here and certainly no cell phones. I had not felt the need to recall her exact words but now, alone in the dark at Lost Point, I needed to recall precisely what she had said.

"You need to come to Lost Point. Promise you will be here on Thursday."

"Is Al dead?" I asked.

"Yes."

"When did he die"

"A while ago."

"So, the final arrangements are taken care of."

"Yes."

"I don't have to come. You can go on living at Lost Point."

"You have to come on Thursday. Will you?"

"Anita, you don't have to leave Lost Point."

"Promise you will come on Thursday."

"I'll be there." She hung up.

These words kept swimming around in my brain as the night wore into a soft morning light which promised a clearing of the storm. Somewhere in the night the lighthouse faded in the dawn and sleep came to me.

Chapter 2

The early light brightened the clean kitchen. The river sparkled and the crabbers in their workboats moved across the surface to tend the pots. Soon the sun would rise high for a glorious day in coastal North Carolina. The view from the kitchen window was comforting but the scene back in the other rooms was very disturbing. I began a plan to convince Anita to stay here. If she would remain in my brother's house, it would postpone my having to make any decisions about it.

I'll call Ed and take a leave of absence first thing Monday morning.

I started to organize my thoughts and make a mental list. I need a dumpster to get rid of the trash, but I must be careful. I did not know where Al kept the money. Most likely Al did not use the bank. That was too conventional for my brother. It might be easier if I started the process before Anita showed up.

The coffee aroma drifted across the kitchen blocking the

musty, dusty smell of the house. I was pouring the first cup when I heard the outside door open.

"Hello!" It was Anita's voice.

"In here, Anita!"

I looked up but it was not Anita. I had not seen her for many years, but I knew this lovely young woman was not the woman Al had lived with for so long. She looked maybe 10 years younger than me—dressed in the uniform of a fisherman—jeans, T-shirt, baseball cap and white boots.

"You are not Anita!"

"No, I'm Jane." I did not know Jane, but she looked like she belonged at Lost Point.

"Jane, I am Sandy, Al's sister. Where is Anita?"

"I don't know. No sign of her when I arrived on Monday."

"She must have been here yesterday; she called me."

"That was me. I let you think it was Anita. It was easier than explaining."

"Explaining what? What is going on here?" The unknown girl did not frighten me but the apprehension from her words caused my heart to skip beats and one of the nagging menopausal hot flashes to travel up my neck.

"Anita is my mother. She called to tell me Al died and asked me to come on Monday. I haven't seen her and I'm worried sick. She left a note to call you. Told me what to say to make you come and take care of things. She wanted you here on Thursday - today." Jane took a deep breath and continued. "I have spent a lot of time getting the kitchen cleaned and food in. You can imagine how bad this room and the bathroom were when you look at the rest of the house. I'm sorry I didn't have time to do a bedroom. Did you make out alright last night?"

"Yes, I managed. Jane, what do you think happened here? Do you know the arrangements for Al's funeral? Where do you think your mother is?"

"I don't know much. But I wonder if anyone knows Al is dead except you, me and Anita. They just wanted to live here and be left alone. I knew someday she would have to call me. Expected it."

This young woman and I already had something in common.

She continued, "I'm afraid Anita is dead, too. A gut feeling—nothing to pin it on."

"Would she kill herself?"

"I've thought of that but where is her body?"

"Where is Al's?

"I might as well tell you everything I know…."

Jane began to talk, and I tried not to lose control of my emotions and mind. It was as if she were talking in a huge barrel. It sounded almost like an echo as I realized that my brother was dead and more lost to me than he had been all these years. That thought was floating in and out of what she said.

"My earliest recollection is living here at Lost Point. I left when I was sixteen…"

Jane lived here? I never knew about Jane.

"About 5 years ago I came back…I don't know why because it was a mistake, so I didn't stay."

She was talking. All I could think was, *Al is gone.*

"Anita and Al seemed to be content living here by the river at the end of the road. So, I let them be and gave them a number to reach me. This was my first call. She said, 'Come to Lost Point on Monday. Al is dead.' I didn't know what I would find but I surely expected her to be here." Frustration and sadness were etched on her face. "I went down to the general store in Aurora. No one knew anything about Anita except she came in to buy groceries. No one knew Al. They did see a funeral hearse in here one day. Couldn't say when. These locals don't say much."

"Jane, I have to know. Was Al your father?"

"If so, I was never told, but what does it matter?"

"Well, if you are—you are his heir; if not, I am. Did you come across any papers—a will?"

"Sandy, I really haven't looked. I haven't been into that mess." She pointed to the great room where the early light was beginning to illuminate the piles of Al and Anita's lives. "I figured it was your job and not my business. I'm not here to try to get something."

"I know, but we must find out if you are…. are entitled. As I see it, we have a couple of big problems here. I am going to call home and take a leave of absence from my work. How long can you stay?"

"I'm a teacher…my summer break starts on Monday. I want to find my mother and I'll help you here if you want me to."

"That would be great. By the way, where did you stay last night?"

"I took the boat out and did some shrimping. I hope you like 'em. Before I left, I was Al's fishing mate on his boat, which he called the 'Lady Jane'. I have been sleeping there. He kept that in perfect shape. Anita was the pack rat in this house."

The prospect of having this younger, stronger person helping with this mountain of problems was reassuring and I was already impressed with her honesty.

As I poured my second cup and Jane's first, a pounding came on the front door. We worked our way across the great room, weaving in and out among the piles, and pulled the door open.

"Mornin'. Is this the Bradford residence?" The name did not register to me, but Jane spoke up.

"Yes, Anita Bradford lives here." It was the first time I had heard Anita's last name.

"I am Jake Stone and I have a bill of sale for fishing equipment, artwork, decoys. It is all itemized and signed by Anita Bradford. Here is the check made out to Sandra Parker."

"That's me." I looked at the invoice and knew that it was everything from the bedroom where I slept last night. A check for $1254.00 fell limply across my extended hand. It took him only a few minutes to load his pickup and head back down Lost Point driveway. Jane and I were still looking at each other in amazement when we saw three more vehicles winding their way to the house. A pick-up truck, the Salvation Army truck, and a big Lincoln Town Car.

The first one was Jimmy Ray Moore, the local antique dealer. He came with a helper and a black Labrador Retriever.

"Mr. Moore, could you keep your dog in the pick-up? I have a cat in here."

In Pamlico County a man's dog was family and Jimmy Ray took the insult as he reluctantly put the dog back in the truck and came into the house to give me an invoice to take the entire contents of the second bedroom, including the furniture. It was itemized perfectly and signed again by Anita. This time I was handed a check for $2695.00 and before I could even draw a breath, another man walked into the foyer.

"I'm making a pickup for the Salvation Army. Mrs. Bradford said all the bags and boxes were marked." Sure enough, on top of all the clothes stacked were tags marked Salvation Army, and the boxes with scribbles bore the same notation. When he finished loading, the only stacks that would be left in the great room were papers and magazines. Meanwhile, in the driveway, a man got out of the Lincoln and came to the porch.

"I don't know what Anita Bradford has for you, but you will have to wait until Mr. Moore and the Salvation Army finish before you can take anything."

"I'm Mr. Hardison. I am not taking anything. I brought you something. May I come in?" Jane and I noticed he had set a box on the porch. He lifted it and followed us to the kitchen. Introductions were managed, and the atmosphere was strained.

Mr. Hardison was not at all at ease with his purpose; his breathing was hard, and a bead of sweat sprung across his lip. I should have known he was not a second-hand dealer—driving that sedan and dressed in a suit and tie, rare in these parts except on Sunday morning or Wednesday evening. Baptist church times. Even then it was the preacher in a suit. Jane offered him coffee, which he declined, asking instead for a drink of water. The quiet of the kitchen was in sharp contrast to the sounds of moving furniture and a barking dog coming in from the front of the house. To make Mr. Hardison's job more difficult, he had to talk over that.

He took out a paper for us to read. The letterhead was Hardison's Funeral Chapel and Crematory, New Bern. I saw 'Albert Kerr' written on the paper and, in an instant, knew he could tell me where Al was. However, I was not about to get information; I was about to receive the ashes of my brother in a lovely marble urn which he lifted from the box.

Jane placed her hand over mine in an act of compassion as I drew a long breath looking at the urn that was shaped like the Capital dome that I saw from my window in Washington.

"Anita Bradford assured me that you would pay the outstanding bill for this, Mrs. Parker."

"Of course, Mr. Hardison. I will be in New Bern first thing Monday to transfer funds and take care of this. I hope that is acceptable."

"A few more days won't matter." He shook my hand and offered assistance, if we planned to inter the ashes, and quickly made his exit.

From the front of the house came a new noise. "I'm looking for Sandra Kerr Parker!" barked the newest stranger.

"I'm Sandy Parker. What's your mission?"

"I have a contract signed by Anita Bradford"... Why was I not surprised? I turned to Jane, and we both began to laugh.

Just a while ago all this clutter was one of our major problems and it seemed to be evaporating like the hot summer rain of yesterday. All I could do was wave my arm to indicate *come on in* to the man with the latest contract signed by Anita Bradford.

He was to clean out and haul away all the recyclable items for which he was going to pay us $125.00. What a deal! Paper, cans and glass. Taking the stacks of magazine and newspapers did wonders for the great room. When he took the cans and glass from the garage, I could see Jane's car parked in the far bay.

"Jane, come sit here at the table and let's see what we have while these people are cleaning out the house." I laid all the invoices, contracts and statements on the table. I had three checks, which amounted to $4074.00, a bill for $867.00 for cremation, and the urn for Al's ashes.

"Can you believe? In less than half a day so much has been cleaned out of this house?" We took a good look at the papers in front of us. The one from Mr. Hardison had another stapled to it - Al's death certificate dated December 14! Al had been gone five months—before Christmas. The Hardison Funeral Chapel and Crematory also noted the date the ashes were to be brought to Lost Point. Today, Thursday May 14. All of the other invoices spread out before us were signed by Anita two weeks ago.

"You know Sandy, Anita arranged all this. She sorted thirty years of accumulation. It was a lot of work. Why did she need us to be here just to open the door and take the money? It really scares me. I'm scared…." Her tears were in her voice. I took the trembling girl in my arms but could not think of anything to say to take away the fear she had for her mother. It had been a very long time since I had embraced anyone.

We sat down to eat a late lunch when a horn blasting the quiet of the now empty house brought us to our feet. It was easy to pass through the great room now and it seemed much larger. I thought someone would be knocking again on the door by the time I got to it, but the horn kept blowing to summon us to the driveway. "Hey Missus Bradford. W'here. Just like we promised - three o'clock. Just wanted ya to know we was out here working." I noticed the Downeast Landscaping and Marine Construction logo on the battered pick-up. Two men were already approaching the house with saws and clippers in hand.

"Excuse me.... Mrs. Bradford isn't here now so you will have to tell me what you are doing." He went to the truck and came toward me with an invoice for yard work to include trimming and removing some small trees and overgrowth, raking and mowing, edging and mulching with pine needles, plus adding gravel to the drive. There was even an item to power wash the porch and sidewalk. "I can't get everything done today. I'll be back tomorrow and I hope Monday morning will be soon enough to get that gravel spread. If'n that is alright for you. Missus Bradford wanted us here today, I had to promise."

"That will be fine. I didn't get your name."

"Lee, Ma'am. Billy Lee."

"Thank you, Billy Lee." I was about to return to the kitchen when Billy called to me.

"Ma'am, my wife is on her way over with the cleaning ladies. They're gonna clean inside the house. Missus Bradford said it had to be today. This afternoon." Of course, this afternoon. Unbelievable! Anita even arranged to have the house cleaned after the clutter was moved.

Now we could eat to the ruckus of trimmers, chain saws and mowers. The house was changing before our eyes. It seemed to reflect a change in lives: Al's. Anita's, Jane's, and mine.

Anita was everywhere and yet still lost to us. She was part of every minute at Lost Point today, but she was not here in person. At least I knew where Al was.

The changes wrought inside and outside of this place caused me to marvel at it all. When I turned back to the kitchen Jane was on her cell phone crying. Her melancholy was contagious. I needed some time to digest and consider what I did and not know about Lost Point. I took Al's death certificate and walked toward the river. *Cause of death—Complications from diabetes.* Of course, Al would not take care of himself. Diet and medication—no way! My brother would feel the doctor's advice would be interference and even if I had known, what could I have done? During these past years, Al's choices seemed to match my choices. That thought surprised me as I recalled how easy it was for me to leave him alone. Lost Point was his place. Washington DC was mine. I had not agonized over him for years and accepted the alone-ness for myself. Someday it would require a family member to wrap up his life. It was now; and I was it. *It-* like the final game of tag between a brother and sister.

I walked around the water's edge and down on the pier where a rickety old bench suited my mood. The weathered boards reminded me of Al. Even the twisted and warped ones were like his life. However, all together the pier was right in color and flaws, in this place just like Al.

The sun was beginning its descent and the shadows of the pines by the house cast long lines across the lawn, down the walk, on the pier and into the water. A good breeze from the west kept the mosquitoes from intruding on my sadness. My heart was heavy, my arms—like lead rods. My head, a useless, weighted orb. Could I will my legs to take me back to the house?

I thought back to that cluttered house where everything spoke of Anita. My brother's presence was not up there. It was here by the water. Al's days were here on the pier and on his boat. I could not make my heavy body move to go back to the house. Inertia trapped me. I became fearful in a rush of anxiety. I was afraid and alone. Fear can be overcome. Loneliness—terrifying. I had no way to overcome that. All chance of reconnecting with Al was gone. I had no one. No one in North Carolina or any other part of the world. I did not realize until this moment that the *someday*, when Al and I would share our lives, was never going to happen. That remote *someday* had anchored my life, my great career and the view of the Capitol dome. The struggle against loneliness was lost. I was alone—as alone as I accused Al of being for years. The core of my being was ashes, just as dull and lifeless as those in the marble urn. What was left was this heavy, heavy body that looked the same and walked and talked the same but was nothing like before.

I took my hands and rubbed them over my face as if putting on a mask. I tried a smile and that worked. With that weird smile on a masked face, I rose to go back to the house where Jane was lost in her concern for her mother.

"I've been talking to my husband, and he can't come. Tom is a Marine and is on maneuvers starting tomorrow. We will have to do this ourselves. Billy Lee and his wife are gone for today. They'll be back tomorrow to finish. Anita didn't pay them."

"Sure, she wants me to cash these checks to pay them. She has figured everything."

"Look!" Jane walked into the great room and pushed the light switch. "We have light. Billy Lee checked the breaker box and reset them, including the air conditioner and water heater. We will have some real comfort tonight…even a bath." That lifted our spirits at least to sea level.

Chapter 3

The teller at the Pamlico Bank gladly cashed the checks and

informed me that I was on the account for Albert Kerr. It was long ago when I signed those signature cards and I had honestly forgotten. "We can cash these checks for you, but you cannot close the joint account until the estate is settled."

"Will you cash personal checks for me on my bank in Washington, DC?"

"Yes. Ma'am. As long as they don't exceed the balance in your account with us. "$19,110.01"

"Well, that will take care of final expenses," I mused.

Jane was wrong, we were not the only ones who knew Al was dead. The bank knew. Something official must have been filed with the clerk of court. There was a lot of money in the account, but I knew it was not all of Al's money. Somewhere he had stashed his part of our parents' estate. He would not spend it for his frugal existence at Lost Point. Three times since Pop died, he tried to give it to me, ignoring the fact that I had inherited the exact same amount myself.

"Can you tell me if my brother had any other accounts in this bank?"

"Albert Kerr only had one account here."

Back at Lost Point Jane was boiling fresh shrimp and making hush puppies. We would have a downeast meal and try to recover from the exhaustion of the day. The shrimp were wonderful, pink and plump, and a side dish of drawn butter and old bay seasoning was beside each plate as well as butter for the hush puppies. I ignored my cholesterol and ate with abandon as if I were feeding my emotions instead of my body. We were full and forcing the last delicious bite when a loud banging came from the front door.

"Mrs. Parker!"

"Yes?"

"Mrs. Parker. I apologize for coming so late. I promised Mrs. Bradford to be here today and I have been tied up. Is it too late to see you? Excuse me, here is my card. "I don't know how these folks lived way down here without a phone!" Mr. Warren said as he wiped his sweaty brow.

"I am Sandra Parker; this is Jane Miller.

"Jerald Warren." Introductions were made for the senior partner of Warren and Warren, Attorneys at Law. "Good! Good! I am so relieved that both of you are here. I am handling the will and estate of Albert Kerr and the affairs of Anita Bradford. I have set a meeting for Monday at 10:00 so we will be ready to go to probate at 11:00. Will that be good for you ladies?"

"Of course. Mr. Warren do you know where Anita is? We have not heard from her since we arrived, and it's been over two weeks since she made contact."

"No. I'm sorry I haven't seen or talked to her for about two weeks, either."

"Don't we need to have her here for Al's will?"

"No. You will understand when the will is read, and her wishes are accomplished. We only need you." He replied pointing to both of us.

The rest of the weekend was spent doing small jobs around the house. I was beginning to feel relaxed as Lost Point became more inviting and comfortable. The grounds look groomed. However, Jane was becoming more and more agitated at the absence of her mother, and I heard her crying at night. There was nothing to do to take away her feeling of doom. How could I give an assurance that I did not feel?

Sunday morning, while I was looking over the bookshelves, an odd object up on the top shelf caught my eye. It was a large metal cylinder with screw grooves and a broken chain attached to the top. It went back on the shelf as I made a mental note to ask Jane about it. It looked nautical. She would know.

Two restless nights and warm days passed. We were looking forward and dreading Monday morning. It came slowly and quickly. As we started out the drive a pick-up was trying to maneuver the ruts to come in. We stood in the yard as Jeff Miner, Boats and Marine, drove in.

"Hey. I'm Jeff and I have a bill here. Mrs. Bradford said you would pay." He handed me an invoice for a small boat and used 5-horsepower engine - $445.00. Dated May 1st. Signed by Anita Bradford.

"Where is the boat?'

"I delivered it here. Down at the dock."

"There is only one boat here, Al's."

"All I know Ma'am. I delivered and launched it for her. With a 10-gallon gas can. Full. Just like it says here." He pointed to the invoice where the gas and can were added.

"It looks in order and that is Anita's signature." I should know, I had seen it so many times since Thursday.

After paying Jeff Miner there was exactly $3585.00 in the money envelope I was carrying to town on Monday. "Jane, after I pay for yard and house cleaning and take $867.00 to Mr. Hardison at the Funeral Home, there will be $2500.00 left in the envelope," I shared my calculations.

Jane moved like a zombie and there was no life in my step as we got in the car and left for New Bern. After Hardison's Funeral Chapel and Crematory, we were off to see the lawyer hoping to find some answers; neither Jane nor I believed we would see Anita today.

Jerald Warren was ready for us. The large mahogany conference table was covered with papers, and a pitcher of water and glasses sparkled in the sun. Pens were lined up and folders were prepared for Jane Bradford Miller and Sandra Kerr Parker. "Here is a copy of Albert Kerr's will for each of you. I will lead you to the important items. Ms. Sandra Kerr Parker, Anita Bradford, and Jane Miller are the beneficiaries of Albert Kerr's will. Ms Parker, all of your brother's assets except the real estate and his boat go to you. All funds at the bank and contents of the safe deposit box will be released to you at probate. The costs of probate and our bill has been paid by Anita Bradford. You see all the figures listed here."

"Yes"

"Go to page 3. Jane Bradford Miller, you receive free and clear the 25-foot cabin boat, Lady Jane, and all the fixings and property contained thereon. The next item is the house. See there." He was pointing for us to read for ourselves.

"Anita Bradford receives the house. The books, the organ and the dining room furniture and other items listed here are yours, Ms Parker. Go ahead and read over the list. Are there any questions before I go on to talk about the house?"

"Since Anita inherited the house, why doesn't she have to be here?"

"Ahhh. A very good question. She has gifted the house to Jane Miller. The real estate transaction is complete." He turned his attention to Jane. "Mrs. Miller, the house is yours as of the deed being registered at the courthouse when the will is probated. You have to pay...let me see...I have the figures here somewhere. The transfer fees and taxes..." We looked at each other. We knew exactly what those fees would be. "Here it is. $2500.00."

"Anita could transfer the house to Jane before Al's will was probated?"

"She was co-owner of the house. She took care of her part and as soon as Albert Kerr's will is probated the transaction is complete." He leaned over to the intercom and told his secretary, "Call Jack Ratcliff and ask him if he could come over here for a minute about the Kerr/Bradford property."

"Sandy, I cannot take this house. I couldn't. Tom and I can't afford to buy your share. You are entitled and we could sell it. I want to be fair."

"No. No. I want you to have it. Believe me. I was hoping to come down here and convince Anita to stay in the house so I would not have to deal with it. What a great solution. You ….and Tom -- I never asked, do you have children?"

"Yes, two sons."

"Well, you and your family can make a home and enjoy the Lady Jane at your own dock. I am absolutely sure. It is right."

Mr. Warren seemed relieved at this conversation—he had expected the worst, and did not like contested wills. A knock at the door brought Mr. Jack Ratcliff into the room.

"I'm Jack Ratcliff, Shore Realty." The grossly overweight realty agent came in, thankful for the air conditioning and the ice water.

"This is Jane Bradford Miller and Sandra Kerr Parker. Explain the real estate transfer."

"It was in Albert Kerr and Anita Bradford's names. She made a contract to pass it to Jane Bradford Miller. The final papers are waiting for the probate to release the property to you for payment of the transfer fees. The cost is $2500.00. You see, she is actually giving you the property. She is paying for transfer and taxes. You will have to talk to a tax adviser; a lot will depend on whether the property is a gift or an inheritance. I understand that the monies paid today belong to Anita Bradford. Is that correct?"

"They are proceeds from sale of her personal property," I replied in astonishment.

He, like everyone else today, had been instructed to be here to transact Anita's business. "Everything seems in order although many things are pending probate, but unless there is an unforeseen challenge to the will, everything will be finalized."

"Mr. Ratcliff, do you know where Anita is? We are so worried."

"I fear she may be dead."

Jane slumped in her chair and leaned on the table. The breath was out of her. I had to ask the question.

"Mr. Ratcliff! Why do you say that? "

"All I know is that she did this and instructed me to act as if she were dead. I am sorry I do not have enough answers, but the whole community has been at a loss as to what Anita was doing at Lost Point since Al died. We know the people she hired to take care of things. Strange thing, she seemed so happy as she worked through whatever her plan was and I think she has handled her loss very well."

"We are out of time, Jack. We've got to get to court." Jack could hardly wait to turn tail and run. In his twenty-five years in real estate, he had never had a deal like this. Anita had paid him more in commission than the price of the house. Papers were signed, gathered and delivered to the heirs. "One more thing. I have an envelope for each of you; sealed as when I got them. Let's go. We can walk together to the courthouse."

We had to carry our folders and our unopened envelopes to court. The proceedings in Probate were anticlimactic – cut, dried, no contest. The will was probated; all papers were signed and delivered to me and Jane. Nothing belonged to Al or Anita any longer.

"I need to call Tom. Shouldn't we pay the $2500.00?"

"No, Jane, stop and think. It is important that those fees be paid with Anita's money so the house is not considered a gift – but an inheritance, if in fact your mother is……." I could not say the word.

Anita probably had more surprises for us, but this was enough for one day. Even with some questions answered, the biggest was still unanswered. We would not have another sleepless night because we were exhausted. I was ready for sleep after we agreed to take the Lady Jane out tomorrow and get away from this point of land on the river. My last thought before drifting off was the difference these few days had made in my perception of the problems at Lost Point. Anita was still missing as was Al's money. I wished we could find Anita and never find the money.

Jane and I had the same idea—to go off alone and open our envelopes, which turned out to be letters from Anita. My disappointment was deep, as I had hoped mine was from Al. Neither letter answered the mysteries. Jane's letter was a mother's love letter to her daughter. Mine was a futile attempt to explain Al's withdrawn nature.

Early the next morning Jane had the coffee ready, the cooler packed and Lady Jane gassed to go. We sat and talked over coffee and egg sandwiches.

"Jane, I was a bit surprised, pleasantly surprised, that the house was Anita's to dispose of. I came here hoping to convince her to stay in it for her lifetime. I am even more pleased that you will have it. I don't need it. I don't want it. Please, don't give it another thought. I hope you don't sell it. Your mother has given you a special gift. She deserved the house or Al would not have arranged it. She also deserved the pleasure of giving it to you. Let's get dressed and go. I am looking forward to boarding the Lady Jane."

"You will come and spend time with us here, and get to know us, won't you? I want you to." I smiled an accepting smile, all the while knowing that it would most likely never happen. This would be my last trip to Lost Point. It was against my nature to go back and build on the past.

The Carolina blue sky and slight breeze was perfect for traveling down the river to the sound. The crabbers were pulling their pots and the fishermen were already on the river. We could see the ferry leaving with cars and people headed for Hatteras on this perfect beach day. Jane started the engine and threw off the lines as I took a seat to enjoy the slow pull away from the pier which, as it diminished along with the house and the point of land, gave me a fleeting familiar feeling of pulling away from life.

"Jane," I called to her over the hum of the motor, "I'm going down and look around Al's happiest place, if you don't mind."

"There is a chest with your name carved in it. Under the chart table"

The cabin was neat as a pin, just as Jane said. All of Al's things were well tended and organized as if each thing in its place expected him to come aboard to go fishing. There was comfort in touching the charts and noting the navigation equipment that assured a safe trip. Rain gear hung on hooks and his boot stood ready. I saw the chest with *Sandy* etched across the top. Tears came as I recalled the year Al went to summer camp and made this chest for me. I regretted not treasuring it enough to know where it was all the ensuing years. Inside, pictures of us as children and Mom and Pop on their 50th anniversary spread out like our lives—disjointed. I fumbled through the pictures, being careful not to let my tears ruin them.

A big manila envelope was taped inside the lid of the chest. Large bold letters proclaimed: *AT DEATH*. A copy of his will slid out along with a carefully written list in Al's unmistakably beautiful hand.

Sandy,
Please help Anita take care of these thing for me.
Anita gets the house
Jane gets Lady Jane
Cremate
Have ashes sealed in an urn
Drop the urn into the sound
at the channel marker # 4

I had finished reading his list when an envelope, addressed to me, fell to my lap. At last.

Sandy, No one knows about the money but you. I never put it in the bank. It is in a metal cylinder on the top bookshelf in the great room. You don't want it but in my final days I have been thinking of you. Please take it. I am no more alone or isolated at Lost Point than you are in your high-rise city space. Take the money and do the things you and Bill had planned. Restore a home and do the animal rescue work you were meant to do. Let me be comforted by knowing you are still willing to find a life worth living. The money is not part of my will. Don't mention it to anyone; just take it. I am sorry if I have left you problems. You have been a good sister. I wasn't a very good brother. I do remember the good times. Be careful of your life or it could get lost. Love, Al

Now, I could cry the hard, heavy crying of grief and loss. Cries for all that was lost to me and for all that could have been. Cries for Al and for our parallel lives. Tears fell and washed thought the grief I had been carrying for seven years. The walls of my life were, like the great room at Lost Point, being cleaned out, cleared from under, and taken away with the love shown by Al and Anita in their choices at Lost Point. How is it that death sometimes makes so many things clearer? Why are values better defined and life more precious and dearer? How does death bring *life* to those left behind?

I heard the motor cut back and felt the boat slow and stop. Jane came down looking for me. "Are you alright?"

"You know, Jane, I am. I have found Al's will, his last request. And he left me a wonderful letter. I **am** all right." I reassured Jane and myself. "Al and Anita could not have arranged their estates any better. You will appreciate the house and boat, and I got the very best Al had to give." Jane could not deny the radiant smile she saw through my tears.

"We have to take his ashes to channel marker #4. Do you know where that is?"

"Yes, it is at the entrance to the sound. When do you want to go?"

"Tomorrow morning."

Chapter 4

The trip to channel marker #4 was strangely gloomy as the grey clouds hung low and the lack of wind made the river smooth as satin. Unusual warmth seemed to belie the day, which called for some kind of cold air. There was no coolness and the Lady Jane gently cutting the satin released more heat under the low sky. Jane and I were hot and gloomy. The grey veined marble urn seemed a bit cooler than the strange summer day. I regretted the choice to wear white as I looked at Jane in her colorless clothes. The whole scene was from a black and white movie of the 1940's except for the small red and green lights that marked the port and starboard sides of the boat.

"I wonder if Anita sold or gave away the little boat she bought from Jeff Miner. I guess we will never know...." I tried to make conversation, but it was obvious and ridiculous for me to wonder about a stupid boat when Jane did not know where her mother was. This foreboding morning and insane situation did not allow me to apologize. We went in silence except for the boat motor and disturbed water.

It was over an hour before we approached Channel Marker #4 and saw a small empty boat tied tightly to the bouncing buoy. It had been tied to the buoy long enough that the wave action had battered the stern. A long blue ribbon tied to the bow caught a slight breeze. I looked at Jane, whose eyes were riveted to the blue ribbon.

"Oh, Jane," I offered my sympathies and gave her time and space.

"Mom," she spoke as a prayer. "Mom" she repeated looking blindly into the waters of the Pamlico Sound. At this moment of realization, Jane did not need or want anything from me. So, I waited.

Jane turned and gave me a small smile. "Al," she whispered.

I picked up the urn to take care of the last thing I could do for my brother. "I would like to come back to visit you at Lost Point and meet Tom and the children. Soon," Jane might be surprised to hear these words as I moved to the side of the boat. She could not know that they were uttered as a promise to Al's ashes in the urn.

The marble urn that looked like the Capitol Dome was carefully placed into the satin skin of the Pamlico Sound with nary a splash. Al went gently, gently down into the river he loved—softly, softly sinking to Anita who waited on the riverbed for the man who made sense of the life they had chosen together.

The End

Beach Trilogy

Too Hot

It was just too hot for the beach. Even lovely, inviting Rehoboth Beach, with its egg white foam and blue waters, was too hot. But she was going to have a beach day, and she knew what to take for such a day on the sand—even packed sandwiches and drinks.

He loved the beach more than she did if that was possible. He could hang there from sun up to sun down and never think it was too hot.

The Delaware sun was unrelenting as temperatures climbed near the record. She knew today was just too hot. She picked up her beach chair, small cooler, towel, umbrella, beach bag, hat and cell phone, and headed toward the water. After everything was well organized on her two arms, she started the trek across the hot sand.

Three steps up the barrier dune and the toe strap on her flip flop broke. She tried to walk on but the shoe picked up sand and made walking impossible. Before she solved the problem with the shoe, she tucked the phone into her bikini bra. Kicked off the broken shoe in the sand, as well as the matching one. Leaving them was not an option. She couldn't litter. She had to pick them up.

Down went her beach chair, small cooler, towel, umbrella, beach bag, and hat while she carried the pair of useless shoes to the trash can. Not easy while dancing bare footed on burning sand. Now without shoes—her feet cooked. She pushed the hat on her head and quickly began gathering everything, while dancing on the scorching sand. A seagull, possibly Jonathan, flew down and pooped on her hat. *Damn*, she said to herself.

Two dancing steps later the hat blew off. Down went the beach chair, small cooler, towel, umbrella, and beach bag. While racing to catch the hat, the phone bounced out of her boobs. Her first audible foul word escaped and shocked a woman sitting near by. She tried to ignore the evil look, glaring from behind the lady's beach read, but she couldn't. The woman looked too much like her own grandma. One moment to apologize and then the hat and phone were retrieved—sandy but none the worse. Slowing down to convince the old lady that she wasn't a bad person allowed the sand time to roast her feet to medium rare.

At the foot of the dune, she opened the chair and sat for a minute. Her feet had to be rescued from the blazing sand. Water from the cooler soothed her dry throat and cooled her feet. It was a good time to apply another layer of sun lotion. She brushed the seagull deposit off the hat and reached into her bra to clean the sandy phone now resting between sweaty, gritty boobs.

Onward beach chair, small cooler, towel, beach bag, and umbrella. It was manageable but the sand was beyond hot. Each step burned more and more. She looked right and left to make sure no one was in range…and let three more foul words fly into the wind.

Ten agonizing steps closer to the cool sand at the water's edge her tanned, relaxed husband got up from his beach chair and asked, "Need help, honey?"

She opened the chair, dropped everything, and dug her feet into the cool wet sand, looked out over the majestic Atlantic and remembered why she came. *Ahhh.*

The End

Shifting Sand

The small, corked bottle on the gift shop shelf held sand, a tiny scallop shell, a miniature starfish, a plastic sea gull, a tiny beach chair, and a beach ball ready to be shaken. And, after shaking, it all settled into an inviting beach scene minus the salty smell, ocean roar, and blazing sun. It caught her eye and she had to have it. As soon as she lifted it the sand began to shift, and she smiled.

"Nice souvenir," the proprietor commented at the register.

"Yes," she agreed.

As she walked back into the sun, she repeatedly disturbed the bottled scene and watched it settle. Sometimes the shell landed on the chair and sometimes the ball was nearly buried. Her fascination was intense, and she held it close to her face. The bottled beach made her happy and engaged her enough to caused her to bump into other boardwalk dreamers. "Excuse me," she said as she sidestepped and resumed her concentration on her own little bit of beach nestled in her hand and held close to her eyes.

"What have you got?" He asked as she climbed into the car.

"A piece of Rehoboth. I hope they went right out there…" she pointed to the ocean and handed the bottle to him, "…to get the sand for this thing."

"Nice," was his only distracted comment as he handed it back to her.

"If you think it was made in China, and not Rehoboth, don't tell me."

Once again, she gave it to him. "You're supposed to shake it," disappointed that he did not enjoy her souvenir. She took his hand and moved it back and forth. "Look at the beach changing."

"Fine," he returned the bottle to her. "You shake it. I have to drive." His mood was evident as he started the car. "Gotta go. Time is running. If we're tied up on the bay bridge, we'll be late."

"I wanted one more walk on the beach today," she apologized. "Sorry I took so much time in the gift shop. Even if we are a little late, they will take me in."

He eased. "I know. I know." And smiled at, and for, her. "Enjoy your little bottle." She appreciated his returning tenderness and pat on her knee.

The drive to Baltimore was uneventful except for the winds and tides in her bottle. Once the seagull was buried, and she laughed. Those tricky seagulls would never get caught in shifting sand. Sometimes the beach ball or shell claimed the chair. Often the chair was turned over as if the wind and tide took charge. The starfish was her favorite critter. When it got stuck in the sand, she gave the world inside a slight tremor to set it free. She developed a technique for building a dune and moving it within its small world.

"Look," she insisted at the light in Queenstown. The scene was perfect—the dune in the back, chair upright, seagull standing by the starfish and shell at the edge of her imaginary surf, and the ball inviting fun. They shared a smile as the light turned green. "Forgive me." She knew he was missing her conversation.

"It's OK. Enjoy. We'll be on the bridge in ten. I'll look at the bay; you look at Rehoboth Beach in a bottle," he smiled. "We'll be there in an hour."

She used her time to stay in the bottle by placing it against her face and looking into it so that all the peripheral things around her disappeared. She studied the grains of sand, the bumps on the starfish and the bright triangles of color on the ball. Finally, when they turned onto N. Charles Street, she uncorked the bottle and put her finger through the narrow opening into the sand. She touched the starfish and seagull. Her finger found the chair and she plucked the beach ball with her fingernail. The bottle tipped until sand spilled through her fingers to her leg—every last grain—stuck around her rings and drifted across her thigh and down her knee. He did not say a word about sand in the car.

He pulled into the parking lot at Johns Hopkins Wilmer Eye Institute and tried to imagine what it was like for her to know she had seen Rehoboth Beach for the very last time.

As he turned off the ignition and reached for the door, she took his hand and held him in the car. "The bottle is empty, the sand is gone but I can close my eyes and still see the chair and ball on the beach. I can see the scallop shell and star fish down at the water's edge. The seagull and his buddies flying overhead, begging for cheese twists."

He leaned back in the seat and turned his body and attention to her. She smiled and continued. "More than that, I can smell the ocean, the caramel popcorn, French fries, and sun lotion. I can feel the breeze, sometimes hot like a furnace blast. The sand, sometimes like red hot coals. I can feel the sun burn and the need for more sunscreen. I can taste salt in the air and on my mouth. I can hear the roar of the surf, the children playing and screaming with delight." He let her go on with her inventory. "The footsteps, bicycles and strollers on the boardwalk, crying babies, fussing mothers, complaining fathers, the flapping of a kite taking wing, the fritz of a cola, the whistle of the lifeguard, even the whisssh of a hand full of sand flying by after the command: 'don't throw…! I can love and enjoy Rehoboth Beach after this, can't I?"

"We sure can." He kissed her.

The End

Cottage by the Sea 2007

The doctor's office was empty except us, and we were nervously waiting for the summons from the a nurse. I turned the pages of a magazine, while he watched the latest war news flash across the TV screen. Suddenly the turn of a page presented a picture of a little cottage by the sea. There it was, like a breath of fresh air, in a picture. A beautiful little cottage with a small front porch and a door flanked by two windows that looked like eyes. A dune rose in the background and the sea oats seemed to move on the page.

It was a strange moment to reveal a dream. "That's always been my dream", I said, showing him the picture. "A cottage by the sea." I do not remember ever telling him of this dream. I was caught up in a feeling of openness and revelation that I need to share at this moment…not later…now.

I could not pull him away from apprehension and entice him to look at this dream with me. He smiled and turned back to the TV.

I went into the picture, sat on the cottage porch, and felt happy. I began to enhance the dream in my mind.

Hydrangea beside the steps are growing well and complement the color of the ocean. My garden snips hang on the peg hanger by the back door next to my straw sun hat and yellow rain slicker. Every wall is painted my favorite shades of white or blue. The kitchen has beadboard backsplash and open cabinets. I heard the ocean, I licked my lips, the salt taste was there.

When the commercial interrupted, he looked back to me and the magazine picture.

"That cottage?" he asked finally giving me attention just as the nurse spoke to him.

"Come with me."

"I will come for you after he has his scan," she addressed me.

My chance to share the dream was gone. They left and I had another revealing and unsettling feeling as I stared at the door he had just gone through and struggled with the definition of the word *gone*.

To shake the dark feeling, I returned my attention to the picture of *my* cottage. I tried to imagine how the back would be and turned the page to see more pictures but there were none. So, I constructed it. I put a porch across the back with a swing so I could watch the waves while swinging.

I saw four rooms and a bath—a nice bathroom with a big tub and a step-in shower. The sea breeze moved the sheer, white curtains. The kitchen and great room was one big space with a dining table by the window. A bedroom and a sewing room. The kitchen and master bedroom overlooked the water. The southern exposure flooded the rooms with good light, especially in the sewing room.

Suddenly, "You can come in now. We're finished."

The nurse drew me reluctantly back. *Why did she say we're finished?* I hate the editorial *we* from health care givers. She didn't get the PET scan—he did.

Holding on to dreams in a sterile enclosure of an examining room is impossible. Nothing invites the heart to go to secret places. This is not a place for the heart; it is a space for science and the brain. That was true because a cranium displayed on the counter did not inspire anything.

He looked into me with pleading eyes. He tensed and slightly withdrew from my touch. My hand stayed and he relaxed under my touch. It had taken a long time for him to allow any small intimacy in front of strangers. The last year had changed many things for us, and I learned to give him a moment to recover each time I reached over to him while in the presence of a doctor. We would not be here if there weren't a problem.

Something on the last scan required this one, with contrast, and as I looked first at him and then to the doctor, I knew a miracle was not going to happen for us today. We could not dream in this reality that would never be featured in a Coastal Living magazine.

"It is back." the pronouncement was made. *It's back. It's back.* Here we go again. All the scientific words that followed were extraneous. He let me take his hand as we got this dreaded news. He could not take it all in; he was still digesting the first three words.

I paid attention to the attack plan on this cancer that would not yield to our hope. My pencil jotted notes and marked dates. "Yes. Yes We will do anything." Even as I was answering for both of us, I knew he was feeling this was happening to him, not me—and I was using the editorial we.

The magazine on the table, still open to my page, beckoned as we left the waiting room without pausing. I kept my mind and eyes focused ahead to our future…. and the vision was staggering.

The taste of salt was gone from my lips. There would not be sand dunes rising behind a quaint little cottage. No swinging on that porch or picking hydrangeas by the sea.

It was never his dream, anyway.

The End

Water's Edge Poetry Trilogy

1.
She Went Down to the Sea,
And watched the tide wash in.
She did not try to count the
sand
As it slipped wistfully out of
hand.
The wave would change the
shore,
Nothing could quiet the
constant roar.
Without reservation of whim
or mood
Nature demands, it is
understood
She wanted change within the
frame
Unwilling to take all the blame
But nature wailed and whistled
back
Refused to waver in its attack.

2.
You Are Safer in Deep Water
The buoyancy there
Is where
The need to touch bottom
Becomes more and more rare.
Shallowness will not comfort
or sustain—
The sand will shift
It has no lift
Waves accost, under handing
The quest to make a landing

3.
Rush Like a Tidal Wave
Sweeping, sweeping—go flee
From within, nothing can save
The wash of pending loss
Engulfing, lashing,
Pulling, gnashing
The plea.
Go, go find a place
Let all woes be replaced
Wet and blown no one to see
Briny tears wash and replace
The ocean's joy
The breath
Of pain from your face.

Eatin' Crabs on the Fourth of July 1909

The Fourth of July dawned bright, sunny, and hot. The sun came up a fiery red ball in a blue sky that had just a white cloud or two floating by to make it perfectly patriotic. The picnic preparations were part of the fun. The chicken was fried before sun-up. Extra ice had been secured and the chest was packed with lemonade and the best potato salad in Maryland. Sam left early for the racetrack to tend to the horses and to meet his friend from Annapolis who promised a bushel of blue claw crabs—fresh and live from the Chesapeake Bay. Dan was quietly making everything easier for everyone. First, he tended to the stable of horses so Papa could feel he was on holiday. Then he moved the tables and chairs under the shade trees and watched to make sure the women did not have to lift or tote anything. He set up the badminton net and horseshoe pegs. Lon Fergus was his assistant. Dan and Lon began to wait on the ladies in both houses, to be at their beck and call for all errands.

Lastly the two workers built a fire and brought the large iron pot to cook the crabs. Papa showed up to give his advice.

"Build the fire far enough away so we can't feel the heat, but close enough so we can smell 'em cookin'." The water was set to boiling and the steam was rising when Sam's *wha-hoo* call announced he had returned with the basket of treasure from the bay. His friend had given him a secret blend of spices in a small brown paper sack. Dan stuck his head in the sack to smell and came up gasping for breath from the spicy aroma. He pronounced it *wonderful*. The live crabs and spices were spilled into the pot and covered. The small amount of water and vinegar in the bottom produced steam that melted the spice and poured the flavor into the white delicate meat of the favored crustaceans.

At exactly noon, family members from the little and big house spilled out to the picnic area as if intoxicated by the aroma of the crab pot. Friends began to come up the hill and the lawn filled with celebrants in white dresses and shirts. It was the only color to wear on such a sultry day. The sun rose unrelentingly. The rays broke through the large maple leaves like quiet fireworks. Laughter was infectious.

This would be a special holiday. The tables under the trees were spread with the most wonderful, traditional treats. All of the cakes and pies were baked by the ladies. Liddy—apple, Mrs. Fergus—cherry, done in those wee hours in the Fergus kitchen. Liddy also made her famous yeast rolls. Gertie and Mama made the cakes. One chocolate, (struggling to hold up in the heat), one coconut, and the family favorite—hot milk dense cake with orange icing. Dan cracked the coconut and Gertie shredded it to make her specialty. The coconut cake waited in the ice chest with the salads so it would be refreshingly delicious on this hot day. Everything was covered by a white cloth to keep insects from enjoying the first bites. The smallest children could not resist lifting the cloth to see the wonders and maybe lick a finger full of chocolate or orange goodness.

Nearby a table was designated for crab eating. It was spread with butcher paper that Sam had bought from Tasker's store. Little cups of vinegar and red spiced pepper were spaced around. There were wooden mallets piled in a basket. Each one had been carved at one time or another by the men in the family. Some were the smooth skillful work of Papa. Some were the rough work of a beginner. Sam had one with his name carved in the head. The Fergus basket had lovely ash wood hammers bought in Baltimore. Mayor Fergus even had one forged of steel and engraved with a fancy "F". From the youngest to the oldest, the art of picking crab meat was refined. Only the tiniest Fergus's grandchild, and the youngest MacGregor, had to be helped with the task. Gathering at this table was a Maryland summer ritual, especially on the Fourth of July.

It was polite to select the largest crab that was in front of you but do not reach in front of anyone else to get a big one. Everyone was expected to raise the crab by the red claw and declare it a *good one* before beginning the process. Eat the crab with your fingers after using the wooden knockers to break the shell. Let the banging and eating begin. First open the crab and discard the inedible and devil's finger lungs. The youngsters had to have their crab inspected and declared clean and ready to eat. Now the job is to pull every bit of meat from every crevice. It would be very bad if your sibling or parent could point out a morsel missed. The finest lump of crab meat came from behind the large flapper and each picker had a special way of handling this *filet* of crabmeat—some went right for it first, others saved it for the last bite. No matter, the spice from cooking, coated the hands and got into the mouth with the meat. Pleasure was written on every face. The families gathered on Fergus hill today knew exactly what to do. The best crab feasts are those where you eat some crabs, socialize a while, enjoy the fried chicken, salads and desserts, and come back to eat some more crabs. This was that kind of feast.

The End

Maryland Blue Claw Crabs

1 bushel of large male crabs (at least 8")
1 gallon water
2 cups of vinegar
½ cup pickling spice
JO Spice* with salt

Stab each crab under the 'Washington Monument' and place in a bucket of clean water to allow the crab to be purged of Chesapeake Bay water. Leave them in the water while preparing the pot.

Prepare a pot big enough for all the crabs. Put a rack in the bottom. Add water, vinegar and pickling spice. Take crabs, one at a time and place in the pot. Sprinkle lightly with JO Spice on each layer of crabs as you fill the pot. Secure the pot lid with clothes pins to keep crabs and steam in the pot as they are cooking.

Place over high flame. After they are fully boiling and steaming, time for twenty minutes.

Remove to trays and sprinkle each crab with more JO Spice.

Invite those who love to pick and eat crabs to the table. All others can eat hot dogs.

*JO Spice is a Maryland favorite, comparable to Old Bay Spice

Hot Milk Cake and Orange Icing

This is a traditional dessert at Watts Family gatherings, used for four generations and attributed to Mom Watts and the ladies: Leevy, Gertie, Julia, Thelma, and Violet. It is treasured by daughters, granddaughters, great granddaughters, and the Watts men, who were great cooks, too. I present it here for future generations to enjoy.

Hot Milk Cake

4 eggs
¼ lb (1 stick) butter
1 c milk
2 c flour
2 c sugar
2 tsp baking powder
a little salt
1 tsp vanilla

(My Mom and I both mix it this way)
Melt butter in milk. Don't boil.
Break eggs in mixer and beat well. Mix in sugar and vanilla.
Sift together flour and baking powder. Gradually add dry ingredients to mixer with hot milk and butter. Mix well, scrape bowl, don't over beat.
Pour into pans that have been greased and floured. Bake 350 degrees 25 – 30 minutes. Check at 25 minutes as oven temperature can vary. Cool 10 minutes and turn out to racks.
Frost with Orange Icing.

Orange Icing

½ tsp salt
¾ cup sugar
4 ½ Tbls flour (Some ladies use 3 Tbs cornstarch instead)
4 tsp grated orange rind
Mix dry ingredients and orange rind well
1 ½ cup orange juice
3 egg yolks
3 tsp lemon juice (Bear Creek cousins added this modification later)
4 Tbs butter

Stir juices and yolks together in a sauce pan. Add dry ingredients and blend well over medium heat until bubbly and thickened. Remove from head and add butter

When lukewarm frost between layers and pour over top of Hot Milk cake.

The Boy on the Wall

*This story is dedicated to all who travel to Ireland
searching for a connection to this beautiful
country and its people*

Prologue

Ireland is a place of walls: magnificent walls of stacked stones gleaned from the fields; majestic walls of cliffs rising from un-relenting seas; walls of mountains holding glacier lakes; walls around green fields minding sheep; walls of ancient tombs ar-ranged to the solstice; walls of high watchtowers guarding for-saken monasteries; walls marking the boundaries of cities that now fall within a modern metropolis; walls keeping people in or out—depending on their political bent; walls of beauty and history. This story begins and ends on walls that hold no beauty.

Chapter 1

The boy with the huge, green, hungry eyes shimmied up the wall to the high window. He did it every day and his feet had worn step-holes that mountain climbers would be glad to have on a sheer rock wall. In 1848, during the Irish potato fam-ine, Sean was sentenced to three months in Kilmainham Gaol, Dublin, for stealing a loaf of bread. If he had been bigger and

169

faster, he could have gotten the bread to his mother and Mary, and they could have eaten it before he was caught. He watched the constable snatch the bread from his tiny, criminal hands and crush it underfoot at the edge of the cottage wall. Sean would be made an example for the next boy who would steal. He was six years old and so thin that the shackle they placed around his wrist could be easily pulled over his clenched fist.

The last time Sean saw his mother she stood in the middle of the gravel road screaming, as the constable took him out of sight. Stealing was wrong, but it was worth getting caught to get one loaf of bread for his mother and sister. They had not eaten since his father, trying to make a living as a carpenter, left to search for wood that washed up on the coast.

As soon as Sean and the constable left, Ma and Mary scratched among the gravel in the road for morsels of crushed dirty bread.

* * *

Sean was cast like a piece of rag into the third cell on the south corridor. Two men in the cell barely looked at him as one muttered, "There be food here, such as 'tis." But Sean rarely got to eat. He was too small, too young, and too weak against the others, to keep his portion. At most he got one bite before it was violently snagged and taken to another bowl. He learned, at his second meal in Kilmainham, to make the first handful as big as possible. Struggling for food was not the only thing that kept the boy down. He was afraid—afraid of the men in his cell who lashed out with anger and frustration at him, the smallest and weakest. His eyes were often blackened, and bruises colored his legs. At such a young age he learned to protect his head and abdomen when fists or shoes suddenly assailed him.

Sean went to chapel and prayed for deliverance—a word he

learned as others cried out to God in the chapel. He wanted to be out of this grey place of hard stone and mortar, this place where death came often at the end of a rope, at the end of a fight, or at the end of despair. Sean wanted to roll in the grass. He wanted to run and tumble into it. To pick and chew it. Sean wanted to do his favorite thing—walk atop one of the stone walls in the pasture and jump to the other side. That would be the first thing he would do on the road back to Derryln when his father came to get him.

Sean did not get out of Kilmainham Gaol. One hundred and fifty-nine years later he was still putting his tiny feet in the step holes to look out the high widow. He was checking the tourists who were visiting the jail. His father could not get him. He was waiting for someone else.

Chapter 2

Sarah Poe Moore was crossing the Atlantic in a luxury liner to retrace the route of her ancestors, Michl Poe and his daughter Mary, who left Ireland one hundred and fifty-nine years earlier. As with all travelers, Sarah was traveling away from, as well as toward, something. The little notebook in her room, telling the family lore about Michl Poe, was her guide, taking her to Ireland.

The ache in her heart caused tears to wet her cheeks as she pulled away from the dock in Baltimore. She had not heard from her son, 1st Sgt Shepard Moore, for almost two weeks. And he knew she was departing on this trip, this day. His email had been her lifeline, but the computer and email became a constant disappointment as she packed to leave. She left without knowing, and feeling for sure, that something terrible had happened to him in barren, stark, brown Afghanistan. Shep wanted her to go. He had compiled the notes in her little book.

Genealogy was his passion and although he could not make this trip, he outlined the places she should visit to find stories about the Poe family in Ireland. Sarah's excitement for the trip was tempered by her worry for Shep.

The ocean was sobering. Its vastness, greater than it appeared while looking from the Maryland seashore. In every direction, she could only see the water and wonder. Did her emigrant ancestor ever contemplate letting the ocean be his final destination, as it invites all sailors, and Sarah in this instant? She stepped closer to the rail so the glamour of the liner and its brightly dressed passengers fell from her peripheral vision. The water did not look menacing; it looked friendly, as it lapped the big ship's hull and splashed gentle sounds and sparkling foam. Her breast and questions pressed against the railing. *How did Michl Poe feel out on this ocean? Was the future as deep and compelling as the ocean?*

"I think I can understand Michl Poe," she said aloud. "Shep is my unknown." Sarah leaned back from the rail and put her hand in her pocket and felt the few dollars she had dropped there for tipping the steward. She had twenty times more than the pound sterling that the small emigrant family had to start a new life. Sarah could get into Michl Poe's scene and, by studying the history of Ireland, get into his situation, but she could not get into his mind.

What makes a man choose to go into the unknown? Michl the emigrant and her own son, Shep. Why? Why did he volunteer to go back to Afghanistan? Why did Michl leave everything to cross this ocean? Michl and Shep became mixed in her mind as she lifted her hands and smashed them on the top railing, breaking her reverie. Sarah returned to her own scenario, rubbing the stinging pain from her red hands.

Going to Ireland to find the family that Michl and little Mary Poe left behind became her mission. Public television, books and travel brochures did not tell her everything she needed to know about this home of her ancestors. She had begun to be plagued with a nagging thought. *Someone* was *waiting* for her in Ireland.

Sarah needed to see this place of magnitude, beauty, and charm to learn what final compelling act made Michl leave his wife and home to cross this ocean. She needed to understand what would make a man decide—on one particular day—that he would go. What about his wife—the unknown person—the unknown name? The potato famine was common knowledge. It was a fact that did not give the human side of the story. Shep had sparked her interest with his research. Now, Sarah wanted to discover why the story of Michl's and little Mary's arrival from Dublin had been haunting her dreams and challenging her mind.

* * *

The wind was blowing and the air had a few snowflakes as Michl watched the harbor lights and surmised they would be docking at dawn. The passage included a portion of porridge each day for him. The child, Mary, was actually a stowaway, which the captain permitted but made no allowance or generous portions for. That was her father's problem. Yesterday morning he got his porridge and there would be no more. The portion was not enough to satiate. It only fought off hunger for half a day. Even so, he saved half of his half portion to give to Mary in the late afternoon. They huddled on the deck of the creaking vessel. That was a better choice than the smelly disease-infested space below deck. So long as he could keep her warm, they would spend their last cold night here before touching land.

Michl was hungry. It was an old gnawing feeling in his gut, but this time hunger was like a passion that he would savor, and for the first time, relish. Coming to America, hungry was good. He was accustomed to hunger and the little girl had stopped crying for food days ago. Michl would feed Mary and make a future, but he had no idea how to do it. Hopefully, his skill as a carpenter and furniture maker would feed them both.

Michl would not look back over the port side of the vessel toward Ireland as if the island would still be on the horizon. He had watched it move away in the first hours of his journey. The green island had been his heaven, and his angels, Kathleen, Sean, and Phoebe, would stay there, planted in the land.

With his hand in his pocket to feel the bit o' sod gritty, he said, "Come, Mary". He hoisted his five-year old daughter onto his shoulders. "We have arrived."

"Be there food in America, Da?" She asked.

* * *

Sarah's ship docked on time with great fanfare and welcoming. The landing was anticlimactic. She felt nothing special as she set foot on Erin Isle. Nothing! Not even great expectation. She was one of thousands of tourists who debarked each day with an Irish surname and a vague connection to this island—one of thousands who hoped to see a billboard welcoming her and telling her where the family secrets could be found. No dotted line would be painted across the landscape, up the mountains, down the valleys and over countless stone walls, to a personal revelation. Sarah was just one of thousands.

Sarah's bags were unloaded and transferred to her hotel where her tour group was already assembled and ready to see *Ireland in Depth*, as the tour brochure promised. Her decision to come by ocean liner rather than fly had, for a brief time, connected her with her emigrant family but now she began to feel foolish with this whole idea.

"I'm just tired," she said to the mirror as she dropped

exhausted onto the bed. Her short nap was fitful as visions of travel, oceans, her son in body armor, and a starving family floated through. Sarah woke un-refreshed. She showered and dressed for the tour dinner and briefing. A quick trip to the hotel Internet found a message from Shep's wife—"no word yet."

The tour director outlined the _Ireland in Depth_ tour excursions to Northern Ireland and the Republic of Ireland and Sarah resigned herself to enjoying the trip and letting her agenda take care of itself. The tour accent on history would satisfy her hunger for understanding the famine and the country. The tour director, in his charming Irish brogue, promised that facts about emigration and the potato famine would give new insight.

Good, thought Sarah, feeling overwhelmed in this environment and unwilling to take charge of her own investigation. She was not well prepared. She and Shep had been online to the Irish National Library to search emigration archives, but the answers she was searching for would not be found in lists of passengers. A huge wall of undefined obstacles loomed before her.

She began to understand what she needed to do. Ireland had to become familiar to her. It had to be part of her experience before she could possibly glean the _depth_ she was looking for. Her notebook, with several entries relating to Michl Poe, would be at her fingertips as she traveled the country and listened to the guide/historian. Her notebook noted—Fermanagh County, Cavan, Derryln, and Dublin. The map told her that these places, except Dublin, were in Northern Ireland. She suspected that Dublin was part of Michl's story because he set sail from the coast just east of the city. The only reason she could imagine for Michl to go to Dublin was to board that ship. A poor country boy seldom traveled far from home, and it was unlikely that he had any reason to travel to Dublin before he walked onto the Mist of the Seas for Liverpool and Philadelphia.

The best plan was to relax, enjoy the tour, and take in the experience while watching for the places that she knew were part of Michl's story, and waiting for that special feeling she was sure would come. If she felt connected or wanted to venture further, she could extend her stay. *It's my one chance.* Sarah breathed deeply. *For Shep*, she told herself. Sarah rationalized and tucked her notebook into her purse.

Chapter 3

Sarah's tour allowed one day in Dublin before busing to Belfast to begin the tour on the north coast. She was anxious to get to Northern Ireland but settled herself to be patient. She would take in the sights and sounds of Dublin today and even resigned herself to tour an infamous ancient jail.

"We start with one day in Dublin and end the tour on the 17th, 18th and 19th, with three more days in Dublin. Check your itineraries. There is one more optional tour while we are in Dublin today. If you are taking all the options, be in the lobby at 10:00 to go to Kilmainham Gaol where the instigators of the 1916 uprising were executed, and the sparks were fired for Irish independence. It is also the jail where criminals and those who stole to survive the famine were incarcerated. I will give a little briefing as we ride the bus. The tour guide at the jail will take you on the 45-minute tour. This will be your first profound exposure to the turmoil that is our history."

The Kilmainham Gaol was a dark and foreboding place. Sarah went there with great trepidation. Who would want to visit a jail amidst the joys and beauty of Ireland? The girl guide was perky, but she could not lighten the atmosphere of an ancient, empty prison that had held Irish criminal elements since the mid-1700s. But it was on the tour. The clouds came and went, and one passed to darken the light that fought its way into the corridor of doors to each cell. The massive doors spoke with a dull solid clunk that would mark their closing. The terrible conditions and plight of the prisoners permeated the inner walls. Piteous cries were echoed in the names and appeals scratched on the walls. Even after three and a half centuries, this jail was not free of its prisoners.

After Sarah shuffled through with a large group of tourists, she found herself pressed against the wall in a small corridor. The cold wall told of the thickness of the stone. The small hole in the solid door allowed the gaping tourists to see the confinement and caused them to shake their heads as they were told that many of the criminals, some of them children, were in those cells because they stole food.

Sarah saw a boy come out of one of the open cells, and before he disappeared among the crowd, he looked at her with large sad, green eyes. She stepped back behind the crowd. She needed to see him again. Was he alone? She lost track of the guide's words as she searched the people for a parent with a small boy—maybe five or six. *He can't be alone.* There was none.

When they moved into the huge exercise room, bright with sunlight from windows up to the ceiling, she scanned for the boy. He was not there. Sarah stood among the group that had moved to the end of the large, white walled room where condemned prisoners were held before hangings. She felt a small hand slip into hers and out again before she realized what had happened. As he disappeared again, she saw the back of his head, his thick matted hair and dirty neck. "Excuse me." Almost without thinking, she pushed through to follow him.

"We are moving this way," the guide stopped her and turned her toward the chapel. "Don't leave the group; you don't want to get lost in here."

Sarah could not argue that point. This jail had already invaded her psyche and she wanted to be free of the oppression of this place. As they took a seat in the chapel and the guide began telling the sad tale of the marriage of a condemned political prisoner, Sarah looked at her hand that was sticky with grime and a thick porridge-like goo. Her hand smelled like the cells she had just passed. Taking out an alcohol- drenched Handi-wipe, she began to clean her hand by rubbing until the grime and goo had been transferred to the paper cloth. She brought her hand to her nose. The smell lingered. She quickly withdrew her hand and stood to leave. *I still smell the cells*, she thought. Aloud she spoke softly to the guide. "I need to go out of here, now!" The guide pointed to the exit.

The fresh air made her a bit heady and somewhat dizzy. Outside the prison walls, Sarah felt delivered. Almost without thinking, she boarded the first bus that stopped outside the massive prison. The bus had its own aroma of packed bodies but Sarah could still smell her hand. When she reached for another wipe the soiled one fell into her lap and although it was dry now, the soil was there. Sarah slowly opened the cloth that appeared to have some meaning in the arrangement of the grime. "It's just dirt," she chastised herself as she refolded it and put it back in her purse. *Until I get to a trash can*, she thought.

The long summer days in Ireland keep the sun well above the horizon and darkness would not fall in mid-June until almost 11 o'clock. At 8:45, Sarah was back on a city bus approaching Kilmainham Gaol for the second time today. She sat on the wall at the southwest corner of the fortress and waited for *God-only-knows-what*. Nearly an hour passed before the haunting, repulsive smell wafted to her. She instinctively raised her hand to her nose. "Arggg. I still have that smelly thing !" she exclaimed as tremors shook her hands and caused her to drop her purse.

The small dirty boy picked up the purse and held it to his chest. He had a blade of grass clenched in his teeth. "Can ye take me to Derryln?" He asked as if her answer would decide if he would return her purse.

"I am not going to Derryln. Please give me my purse."

"Ye are. I must go there, too. Would ye take me as far as Cavan on the main road? If ye do, surely, I'll be with ye at Derryln." He handed her purse over.

"Little boy…."

"Me name be Sean."

"Sean. I am a stranger here and cannot take you to Derryln even if I wanted to."

"Sure'n, we be goin' to Derryln, ye and me." The boy jumped the wall and started to the prison.

Sarah called after him. "What is your last name, Sean?" He pointed to her and to his own chest as he disappeared around the wall of the massive jail.

Chapter 4

It was not easy to make the tour director understand why she was changing her travel plans. She did not understand herself. The decision to travel north out of Dublin toward Fermanagh County alone was foolish and he did not mince words in telling her so. Everyone else would be traveling up the coast to Belfast for the next three-day stop and he hoped she would join them before the group started to Derry. It was necessary for her to sign a waiver of responsibility on her decision. This was the only deviation he would allow. If she failed to join and comply with plans in Belfast, she would no longer be part of the Ireland in Depth tour.

* * *

Michl figured it would take him three days to walk to Dublin.

The road was not much more than a path between villages. Yes, three days usually, but he was weakened by malnutrition. It might take four. "God, please let there be berries," he said to the ceiling of their stone home.

"Ye will no find berries, "Kathleen spat out. "Don't be a fool. There are no berries left on any vines. They are plucked before they ripen." She spoke anger, the only strength she had from a bed that would take her to the grave. "Do not waste a prayer on berries, Michl. Pray for ye soul."

He went to kneel by his wife, knowing he had to leave her and would never see her or this home again. In that moment, sharing a loving gaze with his wife, he lost all resolve.

"Kathleen, I will stay here. 'Tis our fate—yours and mine. God's will be here in this land, in this home, at this hearth. I cannot leave ye." He looked at her and remembered the beauty and strength that used to be his bride of seven years ago—the woman who gave him three children to feed. He could not go, and she knew in that moment that he would sacrifice himself and Sean to stay with her.

"Water," she begged.

Michl went to the cistern and she, with all of her strength, rose from the bed to make sure he went. When he returned with the water, he found her face down on the knife that, although she did not have strength to plunge, went into her body when she fell onto it. Michl took her in his arms with a cry that was animal. "Kathleen! Kathleen!!"

"Michl, "she whispered. "Mary is lost to us. Kiss the ground where Phoebe lies and go get Sean. You….Sean….America, go….for me…. Her husband kissed her white lips as a sticky red river warmed his arms and poured out onto the dirt floor.

* * *

Sarah had a rental car and three days to explore the strange happenings and feelings interrupting her days and robbing her sleep. It was easier to concentrate on the routing of her break-away trip than to think about the dry, smelly Handi-wipe she had folded carefully and placed in the back of her Michl Poe notebook. It was best not to think about that at all. The trip across the countryside took her breath away. The green hills dotted with sheep, lovely cottages and crisscrossed with stone walls felt good. Foxgloves, rhododendron, countless wildflow-ers and heather colored the landscape with happiness and peace. She felt good—the only way to describe it.

Would the boy….Sean make it to Derryln? She wondered as she saw the mile post indicating 90 kilometers to Cavan. *No way*, Sarah was sure she would never see him again.

"What is that in miles?" she asked herself as she tried to cal-culate, remembering that 50 kilometers equals about 30 miles. "That is less than 60 miles but on these narrow roads it will take much more than an hour. Wee more than an hour." she said aloud feeling the Irish spirit coming into her being from the countryside. "And a wee bit more to Derryln."

At Cavan she had a strong desire to stay the night and there was a lovely bed & breakfast, looking inviting, just 100 yards off the road. The sign was swaying in the rising breeze that announced impending rain.

Loaf of Bread Inn.
You are very welcome
Seamus and Colleen O'Mahoney

On impulse, she turned into the lane that led to the large, thatched cottage with flower boxes under every window. The welcome was warm and sincere, and Sarah suddenly felt this stop was important to understanding why she was on the road to Derryln. Her room was as welcoming as her hosts. The fire crackled in the hearth and the rain made a most unusual sound as it pelted the thatch—a hum that was very soothing.

* * *

In another thatched cottage with flowers blooming in the window boxes, Wee Mary was eating an egg atop her generous portion of porridge. In the weeks since the child arrived here, she had regained the rose in her cheeks, but sadness remained in her eyes. Every night after prayers, she cried for her Ma, Da, Sean and the stone cottage in Derryln. She was a small child, nearing her fifth birthday. The famine had kept her bones and muscles from gaining the strength a child gets from running in the fresh air. Hunger and weakness kept her still. The cycle begins of more hunger—less activity—more decline.

Elizabeth opened the door one afternoon three weeks ago to see the girl standing there with a priest.

"Your niece Kathleen and her husband Michl sent this child to you."

"What is your name, child?"

"Wee Mary."

The beauty of the child and the resemblance to Kathleen was striking. Soft auburn curls accented her blue-green eyes. The finely sculpted face featured high cheek bones and a small smattering of freckles across the nose.

It was common for a starving family to search for relatives to take a child. Kathleen thought of Elizabeth and knew that, of her two surviving children, Mary had the best chance of being accepted by this widow of her mother's brother. Her job as housekeeper in the rectory of St Bartholomew's church in Dun Loaghaire meant plenty to eat and a safe haven for Mary. Elizabeth was barren after losing her only child, a girl, who would have been the same age as Kathleen. So, they decided not to send Sean; he was too strong-willed and might be rejected by the woman who had no real obligation to her dead

husband's family. It was Mary that Kathleen, with very little argu-
ment from Michl, sent to Elizabeth. The home in Don Loaghaire
was a world away from Derryln and they mourned the loss of their
sweet daughter, while taking comfort in knowing the child would not
starve.

Elizabeth took Mary into her home and into her heart. She re-
solved to nurse the girl back to health and then travel to Derryln to
see what plight had brought the girl to such condition and brought
Kathleen to the decision to send her. If she waited more than two
weeks, there would be nothing for Elizabeth to see except Kathleen
and Phoebe's graves on the green hillside just inside the wall of the
cottage yard.

* * *

Sarah had hardly settled onto the bed to stretch when a soft
tapping came to her door. "Would ya like to go to the pub with
Seamus and me?" Colleen asked.

It was a good decision. Sarah enjoyed an evening full of
music, laughter, and Irish spirit that caressed her and made her
feel welcome. It was impossible to sit still as the fiddle, the fife,
the drums pulsed a beat into her soul. Soon she was dancing
with her new friends and answering questions about herself. It
had been so long since anyone asked Sarah Poe Moore about
herself. The Guinness made it all so easy. The plate of bacon,
cabbage and smashed potatoes looked and smelled wonderful.
Normally she resisted potatoes to keep her figure but, in this
place, it seemed wrong to leave the neat round of potatoes on
the plate. She ate them and thought of the boy at Kilmainham
Gaol. He looked so hungry.

The music filled the room as the hearty voices of the village
people joined in one more of Ireland's famous tragic ballads.
She learned quickly that the Irish sing of death and parting as

if, only with the beat of the drum and the mystic, sad joy of the fiddle, can the stories be told of those who died in the famine or left because of it. *Maybe I can learn something about dealing with parting from them*, she thought as she spoke her son's name into the din of the pub music. "Shep."

The next song filled the room.

Mich and Kathleen fell in love
As the potato plants were covered in bud
Their love was full of hope and youth
The children came for soothe

The ballad of Mich and Kathleen
Through the winter and in the spring
Go Mich Go Mich; do not look back
Go Kathleen, sweet Kathleen in black

Michl and Kathleen believed in love
When the potato failed to bud
Where are my children; faces like silk
Gone but for a loaf of bread – a drop of milk

The ballad of Mich and Kathleen
Through the winter and in the spring
Go Mich Go Mich; do not look back
Go Kathleen, sweet Kathleen in black

Only God knows what it means
The love of Mich and Kathleen
It is here on the valley floor
And will be forever more

The ballad of Mich and Kathleen
Through the winter and in the spring
Go Mich Go Mich; do not look back
Go Kathleen, sweet Kathleen in black

The land endures; she walks still
O'er rock walls and green hill
O'er red blood on a dirt floor
Kathleen waits forever more

The ballad of Mich and Kathleen
Through the winter and in the spring
Go Mich Go Mich; do not look back
Rest Kathleen, sweet Kathleen in black

By the time the last verse was sung, Sarah knew the refrain and sang the last one with tears in her eyes.

Chapter 5

After spending most of the day with her new friends, Sarah's route took her north again. She had managed to sleep and gather her thoughts. The O'Mahoneys were not helpful with information about Poe family members of today or the past, but she felt her visit with them was the first real touch of Ireland she had experienced since arriving. It was doubtful that her tour could give her more depth than this warm and generous home. They did tell her that Derryln was 20 kilometers further on the road she was traveling.

"Tell me Colleen, why do I see so many abandoned stone cottages with only the walls standing?"

"They are famine cottages. We keep them as reminders of those hard times and as memorials to the families that had to abandon them. Most were homes of the emigrants that went to America or Australia or other parts of the world. We will never take them down and the sturdy stone walls will stand for a long, long time. We Irish have a pride in the famine cottages, for some families in this county are related to those who died or had to abandon their homes."

* * *

There was no time for his wife's funeral. Michl had to go for Sean, so he let friends and neighbors bury her. Kathleen was gone; it was only her body left in this small stone cottage, and her body had really been gone since she went into her final months of pregnancy. The baby was taking all the strength and nourishment they managed to pour into her. Kathleen got smaller and smaller as the womb pushed against her hips. Michl kept his family alive by building coffins for his neighbors and it pained him. He made body-shaped boxes. His payment was the meager bit of food that was no longer needed in a family that had one less mouth to feed. He hated himself when he hoped a death up or down the glen would bring a loaf of bread for his family. He ate less and what he passed to Kathleen, she gave to Sean and Mary.

She bore the girl, Phoebe, on a cold spring morning while the wind was whipping the rain sideways—not a good sign to the superstitious Irish. Rain that could not reach straight to the ground was a bad omen. The spirits were holding the rain from the earth, contrary to God's will. Phoebe came on that cold side-rain. Kathleen cried and cried for her doomed baby. Her tears fell on unopened eyes. Although the mother was young, she had the wisdom to know after bearing her third child, that her starved body would not make milk. The child would suckle but she could not thrive on nothing. What Kathleen did not know was how long it would take for the child to go back from whence she came.

186

"Michl, get Father John. We must baptize our Phoebe, soon."

They buried Phoebe on the slight rise that could be seen from the cottage door. One month later, Kathleen would again lie beside her wee daughter. No one, except God, would know about the knife she had plunged into her stomach. It was easy for the village to accept she hemorrhaged to death—so tragic—so soon after her child died. Michl had to go. He had to go to Kilmainham Gaol to get Sean - the boy was all the man had left.

* * *

The village of Derryln invited Sarah to walk its narrow streets. She admired the walls that rose from the walks in many colors, with flowers blooming in every available box or bowl on every level. The small village had two pubs and little else. "Dia dhuit" the usual Gaelic greeting, was given by each person she met as she walked. To her surprise, as she rounded a corner, she saw the Derryln Museum. It was not open but it intrigued Sarah so much that she went seeking someone who could let her in.

"How can I visit this museum?" she asked the first woman she passed.

"You are very welcome to our museum, but O'Shaughnessy will not return to Derryln today. He be takin' his sheep." She pointed to sheep bunched and moving upward on the hill rising from the town. "It usually takes him a fortnight. Mandy O'Shaughnessy may help ye. I'll take ye to her." In the friendly fashion of the Irish she abandoned her path and purpose to take the stranger to get help.

Mandy O'Shaughnessy was behind the bar at Paddy's Pub. Her curls were escaping the ribbon and her apron could not hide her advanced pregnancy. Her laughing eyes and warm smile were generous to the stranger as introductions were made. "Aye, I will give you Paddy's key. Go and enjoy our wee bit of history. I be right here when ye bring the key back... unless this wee one decides to come." She patted her extended stomach.

Sarah was excited beyond expectation as she approached the museum. Looking at the key in hand, she had a feeling that she had finally gotten to a place she was meant to be.

The museum was a small musty one-room cottage. Plenty of sun lit the dust. The first thing that caught her eye was a large volume under glass. "St. Finbarr Parish Records, Derryln Village, County Fermanagh," announced the card below it.

Sarah had just begun to wish she could open the book when the silence of the museum was broken by the entry of another person.

"A very good mornin', Sarah Moore"

The friendly, gentle woman explained that no one stayed a stranger long in Derryln and word had quickly spread of Sarah's name and interest in the museum. That meant that she must believe she had a connection to the people of the village. Anna Delaney usually made it her business to help such strangers. After a quick introduction, Anna opened her basket.

"Mandy tells me ye were so anxious to get to this museum that ye did no' eat or drink a thing. We will take a moment to get acquainted."

She drew out some brown bread that was still warm and a pint of Guinness that was barely cool. Two napkins and glasses made the picnic possible.

"No hurry. I would you slow down a wee bit," she laughed. "We do no' hurry in Derryln!"

Sarah found the woman and the food irresistible.

"A piece of cheese, too?" Anna invited

After eating a few bites to put off hunger and moving to enjoying the food for its special quality, Anna invited Sarah to tell her story. Instead of telling of her search for the family roots she found herself telling the woman about her son. "Shep was twenty-six last March. He volunteered to go to Afghanistan after returning unharmed from Iraq. His wife, daughter, and I were so glad to have him home and we just could not understand why he volunteered to go back. He said he had to. In truth, Anna, I bought his explanation of patriotic duty and his stand for our freedom and the freedom of the people in Iraq, but when he chose to risk his life and go again...." Sarah could not voice her real fear. "I don't think I will ever understand what makes a man go...." her voice trailed off.

Anna understood her struggle. She busied herself, putting away her basket and the things left from their repast. "Sometimes, something tells him he must go....and, sometimes it is important to know why a man canno' stay", she said ever so quietly. "Does your son have some connection to the search we are doing here?" Anna pulled on some little white gloves and approached the parish records.

"I'm not sure. I feel so close to him now and am constantly thinking that he would want to know what I find. I'll get on the Internet when I get to Belfast tomorrow. Shep was always fascinated by the story of this ancestor, and he wanted me to make this search. Maybe I *am* doing it for him."

Anna opened the case and gently touched the ancient book as if it had life. "We call this a museum but really 'tis just a place to keep this book safe. The church and parish have all moved to Cavan but this book has our history in it. Except for the few antique implements and pictures of the famine cottages, there is not much to make it a museum. It gladdens us to have such in our village. And what would the family name be?" She said as she gently opened the book.

"P-o-e; Poe"

"Oh, my dear, I am very familiar with all the surnames in

this book, and I do not believe I have ever come to that one." The disappointment in Sarah's demeanor was not missed by the older woman. "Let us talk a moment and see what other clues you have. You seem to be so certain that the family came from Fermanagh County. Reading and writing were not great among our people so long ago. Names were often varied a bit. Nothing is sorted by alphabet but if you have some dates..." Sarah reached into her purse to retrieve Shep's little notebook that was guiding this journey.

"He arrived in America November 1850 with a daughter, Mary. She was about 5 - born maybe 1845."

Anna began gently lifting the pages back, back. "Our village is small; it will not take long to look at all the entries for the years you have in your little book. But we do not have departure dates. We have marriages, baptisms, births and deaths. Do ye know how old he was?"

She shook her head and began to believe she would not find her answers so easily. Looking at her notebook, she remarked, "His first name was misspelled. Michael is spelled M-i-c-h-l."

"Ahhhh. Now we have a clue. That is a very distinct name, not a misspelling of Michael. It is pronounced Mick- el. Rhymes with nickel. There are only a few families here that use that name. Let me see....." she began to concentrate on the fluid penmanship of the 1800's. "One thing about the Irish; they are very faithful to the names they use—over and over. That is one of the things that makes finding ancestors so hard." She smiled at the idiosyncrasy. Time stood still as Sarah tried to keep her breathing regular. "We will look at all the entries for 1850 and then go back five years, to look for the child." See here...Death September 14, 1850, Phoebe Pohl, daughter of Kathleen and Michl Pohl. And here we have baptism Phoebe Pohl September 10, 1850 and birth of Phoebe Pohl, September 6, 1850. Sadly, 'tis the whole story of Phoebe," Both women paused a moment in silence for the small baby that they did not know. "I tell you the truth, phonetically P-o-h-l would be pronounced Poe among these hills."

"Really? Then I might need to be searching for the Pohl family. Are they through Fermanagh County?"

"Aye, they are. Here we have the birth of Mary Kathleen, daughter of Michl and Kathleen, December 10, 1845 or 6.

"Let's go forward a wee bit more. Oh dear, here is the death of his wife, Kathleen Pohl. October 1, 1850. Poor Michl Pohl lost his wife soon after little Phoebe."

"I cannot thank you enough, Anna. I am confident I have found the right family." Sarah was making all the notes she needed in her little book. She was sure she had found her family and the tragedy of it. When they found the death of Kathleen just before Michl and Mary left for America, she should feel she had all the answers, but she had a nagging feeling that something was missing in the story.

"Sarah, do you have to leave today? If you are sure the Pohl family is yours, I could take you to their abandoned cottage tomorrow. I know where it is." Sarah did not take a minute to decide. She would stay the night and see the Pohl family famine cottage.

Chapter 6

She was settled in the little room over the pub, listening to the music and voices from below, before she thought of the boy Sean. She had put him out of her mind until she remembered that he said he would see her in Derryln. "He is just a little beggar; I should have given him some coins. I'm feeling guilty...." She went to the back of the notebook and took out the soiled wipe, intending to throw it away, but instead she unfolded it again and looked carefully. There was a letter discerned in the soil. P. *The boy did not put them there—they came there off my hand*, her mind raged. Her voice broke the quiet of the room "This is ridiculous. I don't believe the Virgin Mary appears in tree bark or Jesus' face forms in clouds. I'm not a magician and neither is the boy." Sarah threw the cloth in the waste can.

I am Sean Poe. He is Sean Poe. It is Sean Poe. A voice in her sleep said, as if he were reciting a Latin verb. The voice was Shep and, as soon as her dream allowed it was Shep, she woke herself up. Dreaming his voice scared her and brought her to an upright position with her heart beating wildly. "Shep," she said to nobody. Sarah got the book of notes out and read them over again. She would ask Anna to open the book again; she needed to look for another child. If there was no entry between the marriage and birth of Mary, she would put the idea of Sean to rest—once and for all. Before she put her notes away, she retrieved the soiled hand-wipe and tucked it back in the book.

The rest of her night was peaceful, and she woke to sunshine and Mandy tapping on the door. "Miss Sarah, ye wanted to rise early and I will be having my baby today. Come share breakfast before the excitement begins."

Anna was seated with Mandy waiting to share the fruit, cheese and brown bread on the table before them.

"Anna, can I look in the book again? I think we might have overlooked another child born before Mary, probably soon after the marriage of Michl and Kathleen."

"Aye, we can look but I am the midwife here and will have to be with Mandy soon. I canno' go with ye to the cottage but I can tell ye exactly how to find it. Let's go, times a-wastin'."

In the museum, Anna asked, "Now when was that marriage?"

"1843 or 4."

* * *

Sarah turned to the left where the wall was broken. She followed the road until she came to the bridge across a small stream, passed three famine cottages on her right and stopped at the one and only famine cottage on her left. She knew it was the right one because the mountain rose right behind it, just as Anna said.

It stood alone and lonely. There was no lane, she would have to climb a rock wall. There was something beautiful and lasting in the four stone walls that rose to the sky. The grey walls stood beautifully against the green mountain. The stone had a softness that asked for understanding about all that had happened in the small home. The walls on the opposite ends had the triangular rise that once held the timbers and thatched roof. A doorway sat square in the front and two small squares, that were windows, flanked the door. She went in the door and was amazed that the packed floor had not allowed vegetation to grow after all these years. Sarah walked slowly around the single room and sat on the hearth so she could imagine the family, Michl, Kathleen, Sean, Mary and baby Phoebe living in this space. A table and chairs that Michl had made. Some simple toys and a pot of stew over the fire. Beds that would have to be stacked by the carpenter. Each image that came to her was comfortable. She felt she had found something that she belonged to…and that belonged to her. Time got away and the urgency to get to Belfast was gone. She could stay here for a while. She took out her little book and began to write a letter to Shep. He needed to know what she had found, and she needed to write down why she was convinced that this Michl Pohl was their Michl Poe. She stood to stretch and walk to the back doorway that was off set to the left. In that view, as the yard began to rise to the mountain, she saw the boy sitting on the wall.

"How did you get here?" she asked.

Sean was different—clean and neat—although still ragged. His hair was shining in the sun and his skin was fair. There was no odor. He jumped from the wall, patted the ground, and invited her to sit with him on the green grass. When she took her seat beside him, he took the blade of grass from his mouth and began to tell his story.

"I came with ye. If ye had not come to Kilmainham Gaol, I still be there. I needed family to come and take me home. My father came to get me, but he be goin' in another direction." Big tears filled his eyes and made tracks down his cheeks. "He could not take me home, and I could not go with him." The boy sobbed and Sarah knew, as she knew so many things while in this place, that the boy had not cried since the day he left this cottage. Sarah took him in her arms and let his tears wet the bosom of her dress.

"I be waitin' for such a long time." He put his thin arm around her waist.

* * *

As friends gathered to offer condolences to the man standing beside his dead wife, he did something he had never done….he begged. "Kathleen is gone and I must go now to be in Dublin by Thursday to get Sean or they will turn him onto the street. There isn't much here but all that is in this cottage is yours for putting Kathleen in her coffin and in the ground after Father John gets here." The shocked friends gave him their blessing and a half a loaf of bread.

Michl asked those gathered to step outside and give him a minute alone with Kathleen. He knelt beside her and took her cold hand. "Kathleen, I am doin' what ye asked with your dying breath. I be goin' to get Sean. I love ye. Dia Dhuit." He stood and went out the back door to fulfill Kathleen's other request—he kissed Phoebe's grave and put a bit of Ireland's sod from Kathleen's newly opened one in his pocket. He grasped the bread, picked up a small bundle from the corner and, without looking back or another word to his friends, climbed the wall to the road.

The prison was closed to him when he arrived at dusk on Wednesday. Michl curled up beside the massive door, ate a small piece of bread and tried to sleep. A gentle rain wet him through but gave him fresh water as it dripped from Kilmainham's roof. He was wakened the next morning by an approaching wagon that stopped at his feet.

"Out of my way," the gruff man warned as he pounded on the door. "'Tis Anders, I be here to get the body."

Michl shuffled out of the way and turned to see, to his amazement, a small limp body, with red curls, handed roughly to Anders. "Sean! Sean!" He screamed. "Sean, me Sean. No, it canno' be." But it was.

"This be your boy? Ye can take him and have him buried for a price or I can take him and let the magistrate pay for his pauper's grave. What's ye choice?"

Michl was overcome with emotion; he just wanted to hold the boy—gently touch his bruised body, straighten his curls with his fingers, caress his thin bones, and kiss the face that was Kathleen's. "Oh Sean," he whispered. "My wee boy," he sang and rocked as sobs racked his being. He was crying for Sean, for Kathleen, for Phoebe and for himself.

"Well, what'll it be? I be on my way. He ain't the only one died last night, ye know."

"No money." was Michl's consenting reply, but he did not let go of the boy. Anders had to pull him from his arms and toss him in the deadly wagon. Michl could not watch it go.

His ship would sail on the evening tide tomorrow. There wasn't much time but Don Loaghaire was on the way to his dockage. Michl knew he was going against Kathleen's wishes but he could not take Sean, and he would not go to America alone. He would take Mary.

Elizabeth was not happy to have Michl at her door for Mary. The sorrowful man did not ask—he told her.

"I be takin' Mary."

What could Elizabeth say?

"Me family's gone, all save Mary. We be sailin' for America on the evenin' tide".

Mary, at the sound of her father's voice, ran to the man and threw her arms around his neck as he bent down to her. They would go. Elizabeth gave the man one pound sterling to start his new life.

* * *

The sun was going lower, and the shadows were reaching Sarah and Sean leaning against the ancient wall. "Sean, what is going to happen to you now? Am I supposed to do something for you?"

"No. There be nothin' more. I be delivered and ye be the one delivered me. Ye answered me prayers. If ye had not come; I would never be delivered." He smiled a radiant smile. "I be home."

Sarah sat contented and comforted with the boy until his mother, with a babe in her arms, waved for him to come into the cottage. Just before he reached his mother's arms he turned to her and spoke.

"Sarah, ye canno' stay here. Someone else is waitin' for ye. Go Raibh Maith Agat," he gave the Gaelic blessing.

She did not know all the answers, but she knew that Michl Pohl only had his little daughter left when he boarded the ship for America. He had to go—just as she had to leave home and all her concern for Shep, to come to Sean. Now here on the sod of Ireland she was content to know the cottage was the perfect memorial to Kathleen, Phoebe *and Sean.*

Sarah sat in the shadow of that cottage until evening tide

turned the mountain behind her grey. With great regret, she rose to walk to the rock wall and climb to the road. She turned to take one last look at the cottage of her ancestors and spoke aloud to the scene.

"I am not going to question the mystery in all this. I claim it." A smile was on her face and in her soul as she got in the car to head for Belfast. She smiled because Sean had sent her on her way. To thank him she repeated the phrase she had mastered in Gaelic.

"Go raibh maith agat, Sean."

Chapter 7

Sarah was ready to go to Belfast and join the excursions into the history and beauty of Ireland. Her suitcase was in her room and the light on the phone was blinking. "You have a message from Joanne," the operator said. "Please call, no matter the time. Can we help with the connection?" She was shaking as she recited the numbers that would take her across the Atlantic and give her news of Shep from her daughter-in-law. She was excited, but within her core, had a feeling of calm.

"Sarah! Sarah! Shep is fine. I talked to him today about 9:30 our time. 1:30 yours." The time she was with Sean! "I am so excited. He sent us an amazing e-mail. Can you get online to see it?"

"Yes. I'm so happy. I can get online. How is Sara-Jo?"

"She is fine, but she misses her Nannie. Are you having a good trip? Finding the family roots?"

"Yes, to all. It is beyond my wildest dreams. I have found our family roots and can hardly wait to continue my tour. This is a magnificent country, beautiful beyond all expectation."

She printed the long message from Shep and walked out into the Irish mist to read it.

Dear Mom,

I know you have been worried about me and I know you have agonized about my decision to come back to this land. I must admit to you that I do not know why I had to come back...but I did. It was so hard to leave my women, Joanne, Sara-Jo and you...but I had to. Even as the plane flew off, I felt guilty. Once I got here, I was busy, and the next events came so fast. We went on maneuvers and were in the field for an extended time. That is why you have not heard from me. I was not in danger, but I found myself stranded...for reasons I cannot reveal, but I can tell you what happened while I was in those mountains. I thought I saw a small boy in the distance climbing and walking on the rocks. I went to find him and instead, found a family trapped in a cave by some boulders, evidently dislodged by rockets. Inside a wall of rocks, a mother, a boy, and a baby were trapped. They were starving. I passed my field rations through a small opening in the rocks and got my platoon to come help me get an opening in the wall blocking the cave. It took us four days to move some smaller rocks and make an opening large enough to see the large, hungry eyes. As soon as possible the woman passed the baby to me. She was dead. I cannot tell you how that affected me— to have that dead baby passed from the cave to me. I can imagine how the mother felt when I think how Joanne loves Sara -Jo. The woman wanted her baby to be safe, but it was too late. Evidently the woman starved to the point where she couldn't nurse. We buried the baby across from the small opening in the rocks so the mother could see where we placed the tiny girl with all the reverence we could muster. The woman kept crying - "Sanffi, Snaffi" (the boy's name). She wanted an opening big enough to get the boy out. We were working to get both out, but I cannot begin to tell you what a big job it was—trying to move those boulders with only our rifles as levers. The rocks were monstrous, the wall so thick. We were not making any headway. Meanwhile, the five of us were rationing our food to feed the woman and Snaffi, with barely enough for us to keep working in the heat. Water was a problem, too. We radioed for help, but they could not come to us. Military reasons, you know. It crossed my mind that we might all perish trying to stay here and help this family. Believe me, I thought constantly about my family back home. Finally, we got a small opening to pull the boy out—so small I was sure he would get stuck in it. I can still feel his tiny wrist as my hand clasped them to pull. He came out with terrible bruises on his arms, legs and cuts at the hip bones. She pushed without yielding to his cries. She wanted him out. Things were getting desperate. My men were sick in the heat and our water was gone. By then we were out of food for ourselves. She was refusing any we passed to her. I can still see her finger pointing out the small opening, telling us to give it to Snaffi. He was so needy. Just sat quietly and never shed a tear as he saw the massive rocks and the difficulty we faced to get his mother out. That night I gave the boy the last food we had and wrapped him in my blanket and held him close to sleep. Each night it gets very cold in the desert mountains. The next day his mother was dead. I thought she had died of starvation, but when I flashed my light in the cave, I saw the knife and the blood on the dirt floor. She had killed herself so we would take the boy and go. She did what she could to save the boy—and us. We had only walked a short distance when I looked back at the cave one last time. The small boy apparition that led us to the cave was sitting there. I could see his red hair in the sun and a blade of grass in his teeth. Mom, a blade of grass in the Afghanistan mountains is unique in itself! He waved to me, and I think he said, "Go on" but that could have been the wind. He was gone before I blinked my eye. And now, we know why I had to go.

The End

Faye Green, Author

This short biography will not start with my birth on March 27,1939. It will start with my rebirth as a writer in 1989. Do the math. Fifty years before I stepped into the role that opened my mind and heart to what I always wanted to *be* when I grew up.

In 1989 we retired and moved to North Carolina from my Maryland hometown where I was defined as a student, wife, mother, church and civic activist, pleasant and easy-going woman who fit all the definitions around me. Only my reluctance could prevent my definitions from expanding after retirement. I had time, a home computer, and motivation to write the—*one novel inside of each of us*. And I always had a story for my book.

The idea that I could write *Gertie* (2012), a book inspired by my grandmother, gather characters from her family and the family of my grandfather and make good fiction from it, was naive. But I started. Day after day, I spent hours on the keyboard. Even when I was in my gardens or out on our boat, the story was working in my mind. Often, I would wake at night or early morning to get something down that had come to mind. It is hard to say when I became transfigured into something new, but I became a writer. It happened during those early retirement years. It happened when no one had read a word. It happened before any of my books were published. It happened before I admitted to myself what and who I had become. No one saw this manuscript. For many years I typed,

I reviewed, I rewrote, and I put chapters in the desk drawers. For many years, I tried to be what I had always been, nothing more, nothing less, and certainly not a published author.

Sometimes a major event in life causes one to move out of one's comfort zone. I was certainly comfortable putting my writing efforts in the desk drawer until I moved from North Carolina to Delaware in 2004 and a new friend asked, "What do you like to do in your spare time." I told her. She insisted I let her read my chapters. She was the first reader. Both my husband and mother passed away without reading my pages. Sad, but true. My friend insisted I finish the book. She constantly asked for more chapters. She demanded I get it published. What a friend!

It may appear that I wrote and wrote and published, but I did not. Life got in the way in 2005 when my husband became very ill. Time was not mine and neither was concentration. Living one day at a time in his crisis does not lend itself to creative thinking. It was not until 2008, while I was trying to figure out how to live alone after a long happy 47-year marriage ended so tragically, that I went back to the keyboard.

I love to write. I love to meet my characters repeatedly at the keyboard. I love the emotions we share—the tears and the joys. I love to go into the scenes I create and move events through them. When writing, I am at another time and space. If I can make the story seem real there is joy in coming back to it each day to write again. I am never disappointed by my characters! If they are good, bad, or irrational in my mind, I assure you, they will act accordingly on the page. More importantly, I miss the characters when the book is finished. Terribly.

In 2012, I published. My words were out of the drawer and out of the computer files. They were subjected to the proofer's notes and editor's red ink. They were printed, bound and open to scrutiny, review, and criticism. The osmosis was complete. Good or bad, I had become—Faye Green, Author

The most asked question is 'how do you come up with your ideas?' As long as I can remember, I have created stories from events. I can write a story with a prompt or inspiration. Now it is called Flash Fiction. I was writing flash fiction long before it had a name or became a genre.

I often write short stories or non-fiction essays when some emotion becomes compelling. Often the inspiration comes in the midst of drama or a quiet truth that seeps into me. I sometimes have to leave one manuscript to get a new idea written down. I cannot explain it. Once in 2009, I was writing two novels at one time.

Poetry is required of a novelist, according to Edgar Allan Poe. In one of his essays, he doubted a good writer could successfully create unless poetry is part of his expression. Poe also said that every word must lead to the author's desired outcome. I try to do that.

A story can be based on my experience but not always. Imagining how I would feel prompts all of my writing. The shorter pieces went into my drawer file or were hidden among hundreds of computer files. This year I decided to pull them out, rewrite, edit, and list them on a table of content. Not because as a whole they paint a cohesive picture, but because they are pieces and edges of me. I intended to name this book *Pieces & Edges* but as I brought it together a new title—*Close to Home*—came, demanded, and insisted—just as many ideas do!

Close to Home (2023), A Collection of Stories, Memoirs, Poems and Recipes by Faye Green is my seventh published work. Each piece in the table of contents is centered on me in some way, even the fiction. My children and my sister will be able to see how *close to home* they are. I hope each reader will find a personal connection to me in at least one or two of them.

Thank you for reading,

Faye

Acknowledgments

A few short lines in a newly published book hardly express the importance of those who have helped the author arrive at this day.

Bill Byer, husband extraordinaire, has given all his attention, whenever I needed it, to my writing efforts. His expert proofing eye and the hours he spent reading and re-reading my pages are beyond measure. And, he tells me *I'm great!*

Judy Reveal is MY editor. Her comments and insight are right-on. She gives me confidence to hand my work to the publisher. I look forward to working with her on the next book. It is a pleasure.

It is time to thank (officially) the team at Salt Water Media—MY publisher. We have worked together on three books, and I will not take my work to any other. *Close to Home* was especially challenging with all my peculiarities on form and cover. Stephanie Fowler stayed with me, worked with me, and laughed with me until my vision for this very different book was accomplished. Kudos to Stephanie, Patty Gregorio, and Andrew Heller. It is always good to walk into your office.

www.ingramcontent.com/pod-product-compliance
Lightning Source LLC
Chambersburg PA
CBHW031407250626
47155CB00004B/1443